BURY GRAMMAR SC

Jo King

Time Traveller

DATE DUE

Sarah Garrett

Illustrated by
John Lightbourne and Geraldine Mitchell

Seven Arches
Publishing

Published in November 2010
By Seven Arches Publishing
27, Church Street, Nassington, Peterborough PE8 61QG
www.sevenarchespublishing.co.uk

A catalogue record for this book is available from the British Library.

Cover design, scans and typesetting by Alan McGlynn.

Printed in Great Britain by imprintdigital.net

ISBN 978-09556169-9-0

For my brother Stephen Horne whose chorister's solos were always perfect.

‹IF THIS IS THE FIRST TIME YOU HAVE READ ONE OF THE BOOKS THAT RECORDS THE ADVENTURES OF CHILDREN FROM THE TWENTY FIRST CENTURY IN A TIMEZONE DIFFERENT TO TODAY. YOU NEED TO KNOW›

> That SHARP stands for The Scientific History and Art Reclamation Programme.

> That STRAP stands for the Scientific Testing and Recording of Aggression Programme.

> That time slip is something that you might suffer if you travel through time and space, in a similar way to how some people get jet lag when they fly long distances on a jet air liner.

> That if you travel through time and space you are a xrosmonaut.

CHAPTER 1

The Court Of The Chorister

A brand new ride cymbal was the latest addition to Jo Kelly's drum kit and her drumsticks were hitting it now with an angry intensity. At the same time, Jo drove her foot down hard on the kick drum pedal, so that a low boom resonated throughout the house. Soon her hands were flying rhythmically between the snare drum, the crash cymbal and the high hat, transforming the entire kit into a single instrument of protest. She *would* show them. Smash! She *would* get their attention. Bang! She *would* make herself heard. Boom!

'Josephine!' her father shouted from within the depths of his study, 'if you're going to make such a racket, please shut the door!'

'It is shut, Dad!' Jo yelled back. 'I have to be allowed to practise too you know!'

As if in response to this, Jo's door opened and her mother, Dr Harriet Kelly, peered round.

'That doesn't sound like practising to me, Josephine,' she said stiffly, allowing only the slightest trace of disapproval to register in her voice. 'It sounds as if you're trying to drown the boys out.'

Jo laid her drumsticks to rest and smiled innocently at her mother.

'It isn't my fault they just banned me from the living room. I was putting them off – apparently. And I was only making Christmas decorations.'

'You can do what you want in the living room very soon, darling – the boys will be going off to rehearsal in college. But you know how much practice choristers have to do in the run up to Christmas.'

'And what about *my* practice – for *my* gig? My band are performing at the Christmas Sparkle Disco in a couple of weeks – remember?'

'Oh yes, tha...t,' Harriet paused. 'I'd forgotten about that.'

'Surprise, surprise,' Jo muttered under her breath.

If Harriet Kelly heard this remark, she decided to ignore it.

'I'm sure the Sparkle thingy will be wonderful, Josephine, but you do know what I mean. It's not the same, is it?'

'Oh I do know!' Jo said emphatically. She then started to imitate her mother's cultured tones with: 'the Magdalen College Choir has centuries of tradition to uphold! A reputation to sustain! High standards to maintain!' She looked at Harriet with a challenge in her eyes, then continued in her own voice: 'Blah, blah, blah. But if *I* mess up, no one will even notice. Or care.'

'That's not fair, darling,' Harriet replied gently. 'Of course we care.'

'Grandma was right,' Jo said, a touch of bitterness creeping into her voice. 'I'm living in the Court of the Chorister!'

Harriet raised an eyebrow.

'Grandma said *that*? I'll have to have a word with her.'

Mother and daughter fell silent for a few moments, and as if on cue, the ethereal sound of choir-boys singing floated into the space. The tension in Harriet's face evaporated at once, and her expression relaxed into one of happy approval.

'Now, *that's* what I call music.'

Jo whipped a drumstick down onto the crash cymbal in reply so that Harriet's hands shot up to cover her ears.

'That's enough!' Harriet was angry. 'No more drumming! Do you understand?'

Jo's father, Professor Matthew Kelly, chose this moment to emerge from his study and join his wife

3

and daughter in Jo's room. He looked as if he was gearing up to play his traditional role as family peacemaker.

'Couldn't help overhearing some of your conversation,' he said politely. 'How about we allow Josephine back into the living room to carry on making her decorations? The boys will cope. Josephine, you can be their audience.'

'Thanks, Dad.' Jo had won a small victory.

'Well, alright then,' agreed her mother.

Professor Kelly gave his daughter a conspiratorial wink before disappearing once more into his study. Jo caught a glimpse of him vanishing back into his room before he shut his door, quietly but firmly.

'That's that then. Won't see Dad again for hours now,' Jo said sadly.

Harriet's manner towards her daughter softened momentarily. She put her arm affectionately round Jo's shoulder.

'Let's listen in the lounge together,' she suggested, 'and I'll help you with the decorations.'

'Promise?' Jo said, brightening up. 'But what about your students? Don't you have tons of their work to mark?'

'Marking will have to wait a bit longer, won't it?'

her mother replied.

For the first time that day, Jo gave her mum a genuine smile.

As they entered the living room together, a blast of cold air hit them. The window was wide open, letting in the bitter chill of the December air. Jo's ten-year-old brother, Oliver, was standing right in front of the open window, flanked on either side by his two best friends, Ross and Gabriel, and the three of them were singing choral music at the tops of their voices; the sound flooded out of the house and away into the streets beyond. Jo could almost imagine the music flowing through their city, the city of Oxford, like a pure but powerful stream of silver. The boys finished the piece with a triumphant chord in three-part harmony and Harriet applauded enthusiastically.

'Magnificent!' she exclaimed. Then she walked over to the window. 'But do you *have* to have the window open? It's freezing in here! What happens if you catch colds?'

'We can't possibly have our celebrity choirboys croaking out their solos in the run-up to Christmas, can we?' Jo chimed in.

Oliver pulled a face at his sister.

'You know, Mum, the best place to sing in the

house is the living room …' he began, but before he could finish the sentence, Jo, Ross and Gabriel jumped in to finish it for him:

'…with the window open, so it has somewhere to go!' they chorused.

'So you keep saying,' Harriet replied. 'But you will have wasted all these hours of practice if you're too ill to sing in college. That will get me into trouble with your Informator Choristarum.'

This was the grand title that Oxford's famous Magdalen College School Choir gave to its choirmaster – an ancient title that reflected the fact that its choir had been run along the same lines since it was founded in 1480.

'I think his majesty, the Informator Choristarum, might also be interested to know that I saw the three of you pigging out on the chocolate Christmas tree decs,' Jo put in. 'And I thought you weren't allowed chocolate before a service, especially at this time of year.'

'Boys!' Harriet explained. 'You know chocolate coats the throat! What's got into you?'

'Sorry, Dr Kelly,' muttered Ross and Gabriel. They looked uncomfortable. Oliver, on the other hand, turned his face away from his mother so that she couldn't see him sticking his tongue out at Jo.

'What's it worth eh, Ollie?' she taunted him back. 'How much will you boys pay me for not informing on you to your precious Informator?'

'Oh really, Josephine,' her mother grumbled. 'You're being stupid.'

Harriet fussed over the boys, reminding them to put on warm jumpers and checking Oliver's temperature, before shutting the window with a defiant bang.

'Goodness! Is that the time already?' she said, checking her watch. 'It's Saturday – we've got two o'clock rehearsal in college, then six o'clock Choral Evensong. We need to leave now!'

And that was that. Harriet barely gave her daughter a second glance as she ushered the boys out of the living room and away to the hall to get their coats, hats and gloves on. Jo was left alone, her mother's promise to help her make decorations totally forgotten.

Jo glanced sadly at the silver and gold stars that she had cut out earlier, now in a pile under the tree, together with green crepe paper, tinsel and glitter, all ready to be transformed into the magical trappings of Christmas. She dragged the stuff out and started half-heartedly to continue with the garland she had planned. But it was no good. She felt completely deflated. She shoved the stuff back where it had been, one star escaping and landing in the middle of the living room carpet. She left it there and marched back up to her room.

She could go up and play her drums but her spirits were too low even for drumming – she needed somebody, anybody to make her feel she mattered. She reached for her mobile, her lifeline to her friends and to the one person who understood her, Grandma. She had been brought down twice in one day: her mother hadn't given a second thought to breaking her promise to her which was almost as bad as the humiliation of being banned from her own living room by her *younger* brother!

She keyed in the number of one of her best friends.

'Hi Emily, are you busy.'

'Jo? That's weird I was just about to call you. Can you come out this afternoon?'

'You bet. Only I'll have to ask Dad. What were you thinking of doing?'

'Have you forgotten the humanities' project.'

'Of course!'

On Friday there had been a half-hearted discussion about getting together the next day in order to do the project: it involved visiting Oxford's museums.

'When we've finished we can chill out – get a hot chocolate at the café in the covered market, enjoy ourselves,' burbled Emily before saying she would ring Ruby, the third person in their trio and see if Ruby's mum or gran would drive them into the city.

Jo, now a whirlwind of energy, yanked open drawers, pulled out various hooded tops, discarding several until she came to the right one, stuck a woolly hat on her head and wound a scarf round her neck, all self-pity forgotten. After getting an absent-minded assent for her afternoon's activities from her father, no doubt glad that she was no longer going to be playing her drums, she was ready to leave the house.

But first she had a text to send to a special person – her father's mother, Shirley, who lived in Brighton:

'non-person in court of choristers seeks luv and understanding from the only one who understands'

The reply came back quickly:

'hold yr head high, remember theres nothing cooler than a girl drummer luv always grandma xxx'

CHAPTER 2

The Girl In The Museum

'I'm beat,' moaned Jo as she pulled off her shoes and stretched her legs out under the café table in Oxford's covered market. 'Three museums in two hours! Never again.'

'And whose fault is that?' Emily asked. Emily, as well as being one of Jo's two best friends, was the singer in Jo's band. She was also the group's self-appointed spokesperson and leader. Now, she narrowed her eyes meaningfully at Jo and stirred her hot chocolate with studied care. 'Who can always be counted on to leave their assignments till the last possible minute?'

Ruby, Jo's other best friend, the band's keyboard player and the other person sharing the table, put her hand up and gave a tongue-in-cheek performance of a submissive student.

'Please, Miss…so sorry, Miss. Confession time. I haven't started the assignment yet either!'

Emily pulled her shoulders back and sat up straight. 'This will not do, Year 8, Humanities group, set 1c. I am profoundly disappointed in you. You've had three weeks to get to grips with this assignment: 'Compare and Contrast Three of Oxford's Museums'. You live in Oxford. You are surrounded by history and culture. This should have been the easiest of assignments. What can possibly be your excuse? What went wrong?'

Ruby gestured at the Christmas tree in the corner of the café and then at the coloured fairy lights strung across the café entrance. 'There's my excuse, Miss. It's December. Christmas is a full-time job: presi lists, cards to write, decs to put up…'

'…And shopping,' Jo put in. 'Don't forget the shopping. Shopping, shopping and then, just when you thought it was over, a bit more…'

'*SHOPPING*!' all three girls chorused. The three of them started laughing – giggling together the way they nearly always did.

Then Emily stopped and shook her head. 'So we know what you two will be doing this evening then. Writing up! An afternoon's whirlwind dash around the Ashmolean, The University Museum of Natural History and the Pitt Rivers, with Ruby's poor gran trying to keep up so as to keep an eye on us for the mums, followed by the dreaded…' she paused and lowered her voice for dramatic effect, 'the dreaded all-night essay crisis. Shame though. Bang goes our band rehearsal time for the disco. And we do still need to practise, don't we? We're not ready for that gig yet.'

Jo thought, but didn't say, that the only person who needed more practice was Emily: sadly, her singing wasn't quite up to scratch. Ruby, always outspoken, came out with it, though.

'We've nailed the instrumentals, Em. But maybe it's you who needs a bit more rehearsal time. Your vocals need more work. What about a few tips from Jo's brother perhaps?'

'Actually,' Emily retorted. 'If those uptight musical purists would take girls, I'd have auditioned for his choir ages ago…or Christ Church. Or New College.'

'Well, aren't all-male choirs the biggest, coolest boy bands in the world?' asked Ruby.

'And, Em, there's Westminster, Canterbury and Kings to blame as well,' Jo joined in laughing.

Emily's face was serious. 'Aren't any of them taking girls yet? How is that legal? Equal ops, and all that? Why should boys get the best singing tuition? Tuition that's not available to girls. It's incredibly unfair! I'm going to check out the implications for these all-male choirs. Take it to the top – the European Court of Law, no less.'

'Oh really, Em,' groaned Ruby. 'Isn't the whole point of them tradition? They want the sound they make to stay the same: the way it has for centuries.'

'Not if I can help it. I'm going to take them on.' Emily's face set itself into its most stubborn frown, making her friends laugh.

'You're starting to sound like me, Em, when I go off about how unfair it is Ollie gets all the attention,' said Jo. 'And Ruby – you're starting to sound like my mum – *the way it has for centuries!*' etcetera. Her whole universe revolves around my annoying little brother and his boring old choir.'

'Hey, talking of choirboys,' Ruby broke in, 'isn't that Stuart Jones? Didn't he used to be head chorister at the *other place* – your brother's big rivals? Before his voice broke?'

Without making it too obvious, Ruby gestured in the direction of a table further back in the café where a boy of fourteen was sitting, obviously watching them.

'An aspiring King of Cool,' said Jo. 'Check it out: black jacket – skinny white jeans – grey shirt.'

'Neat,' said Emily.

'Very neat,' said Ruby.

'Wait for it,' said Jo. 'Any minute now he'll be putting on designer shades.'

'Showing signs of strain, though, if you ask me,' said Emily. 'Look at the way he's sitting – you know almost too casual, like he's in an advert or something. Yeh...way too casual, if you know what to look for.'

'And you do?' Jo laughed. 'Well I suppose you are

our resident boy expert.'

Emily, with long, straight, fair hair and blue eyes, always had boys interested in her; her pretty uniform features were what boys liked. Ruby with an English dad and Indian mum was, Jo thought, lovely in a more original way. But Ruby was most comfortable in track-suit and trainers, and after school would rush off to play football or any other sporting activity going. Jo was the same, with a touch of the tomboy about her, happiest in jeans and tops, her long light brown hair usually worn tied back.

At that moment, Emily made eye contact with Stuart and flashed him a dazzling smile, while still managing to talk about him with her friends.

'My guess is he's been waiting for a date. But the date hasn't shown up, so he's a bit stressed. On the out-side, looking cool. But underneath, the usual mess of hormones and self-doubt.'

'Just like any other fourteen-year-old boy then,' said Ruby.

'Yes, but ex-head choristers have experienced celeb treatment. He won't appreciate having been stood up.'

'Who does, Em?' asked Jo. 'Not that I've been on any dates yet to know what it's like being stood up.'

'Me neither,' said Ruby.

The girl's conversation was cut short as Stuart got up from his table and came over. To Jo's irritation, Emily's manner immediately changed.

'So, you've decided to join us?' Emily's eyes were flirting.

'Why not? Look's like my friend's a no–show.' Stuart turned to Jo. 'I remember you. Aren't you Oliver Kelly's sister? How's he coping with the pressure at Magdalen?' Stuart pulled out a chair and sat down.

'Well, what can I say? It's December and you know what that means!'

'Poor kid,' Stuart nodded. 'Chorister melt-down season. I still wake up in a cold sweat remembering that Christmas build-up. The terror of blowing those Christmas solos!'

'Bet you miss it though,' said Emily. 'We're all dead jealous of Ollie.'

Stuart smiled in agreement. 'I don't think I'll ever be as famous as I was at thirteen, that's for sure. But now, we all still get to go back to the Dean's house at Christmas.'

'And what do you do then?' asked Ruby. 'More singing?'

'God no,' said Stuart. 'Just daft games, but they're

really funny because we spoof them up. Stuff like murder in the dark, sardines, treasure hunt, wrapping each other up in toilet paper as mummies.'

'Toilet paper!' exclaimed Emily. 'Hardly what I'd associate with angelic choirboys. Don't shatter my illusions!'

'You'd be surprised!' Jo said. 'They're not so angelic are they Stuart? You are Stuart Jones, aren't you?'

'Yep, I am.'

'And as you guessed, I'm Ollie's sister. My name's Jo and these are my mates, Emily and Ruby.'

'Pleased to... as they say. I thought I remembered you all from way back. What you are you guys up to?'

'Well, apart from these two being behind on our humanities assignment,' said Emily, 'we've formed a band. And my band members were just saying that I could use a few singing tips from a real choirboy – and then right on cue – you show up.'

'Ex-choirboy,' Stuart corrected her. 'I can't sing treble any more. And I'm not sure choirboy stuff is relevant for you if you're singing in a band. How's it going to help you to know about the knack of carrying a candle?'

'Which is?' asked Ruby, intrigued.

'Basically it involves a firm grip,' Stuart grinned,

grasping a spoon tightly in one hand to represent the candle. 'You mustn't move your hand around and you must keep it on the exact level with the candle of the person adjacent to you.'

'Sounds dead tricky to me,' said Ruby.

'Actually it is.'

'What other nuggets of wisdom can you share with our lead singer?' she asked.

'Well, our kind of singing needs a straight back and a straight neck. It's important to look and sing up and out never at the congregation. And not to shift your weight about because the swaying is more noticeable than you think…see what I mean? Hardly useful stuff for a would-be rock chick, is it?'

'Shame,' said Emily. 'I could use some inspiration. I'm not quite cutting it as a lead singer.' Emily looked a little accusingly at her friends. 'Apparently.'

'Guess I can pass on one essential tip,' Stuart said. 'Key thing for all singers – across the board.'

Stuart waited for a moment, confident that he had a captive audience. 'It's all in the warm-up. Vocal exercises, a gentle jog round the park, meditation – whatever works for you. But the warm-up, the preparation: it's everything. You have to *get into the zone*.'

'What was your warm up then?' asked Emily.

'Every choir works differently,' Stuart replied. 'But I think we had some pretty unique methods. This is on a strictly 'need to know' basis, right?'

The girls nodded.

Jo was wondering if Stuart might be about to tease Emily with some sort of crazy story but she kept quiet. She could tell that Stuart was enjoying the girls' attention; he was just getting into his stride.

'Picture this,' he said lowering his voice to a whisper. 'We've come into chapel ready for afternoon rehearsal, still hot and sticky from playing a football match. Then we all get togged out in our ruffs and cassocks, sitting round in a circle on the floor. No choirmaster yet, just the verger. And it's this chap who has control at this point. He starts off telling some bad, really, really non–funny jokes. Like: how do you stop a rhino charging? Answer: take away his credit card. Some of the little tykes laugh and us older ones just roll our eyes.'

'And then?' asks Ruby.

'Well even though the jokes are bad, we start relaxing just laughing at how bad they are. Laughing is good – it makes you relax. Anyway the verger had placed speakers strategically round the chapel. So he brings in the rock 'n roll – best kind of music to get us into the zone: gets rid of inhibitions. And here we are before the choirmaster's turned up – sitting in a circle in the darkening chapel. Hushed choirboys, fading afternoon light struggling to filter in through the stained glass windows, candles flickering quietly.' Stuart's voice was getting quieter and quieter and the girls were listening more and more intently.

'And then, **KER BOOM**!' Stuart almost shouts, and the girls jump. 'Verger hits the play button on the CD. A tidal wave of sound! Maybe Nirvana, Maybe the Raconteurs, maybe Dead Weather. Whatever. Can you imagine 'Smells Like Teen Spirit' ever sounding the same in your bedroom after you've heard it racketing around in a huge space like the chapel when the light is just fading?'

'Legend!' exclaimed Ruby and Emily.

'I don't think that would be allowed in Magdalen,' said Jo, imagining how horrified her mother would be at the thought.

'Then,' Stuart went on, 'we'd be up and dancing – cassocks flying in all directions, heads thrashing, punishing our air guitars, mouthing the words at each other. The verger joined in – black robes shaking, till suddenly he hits the stop button. He always knew the right moment. Just before the choirmaster was going to make his grand entrance. And sure enough, in he comes. Then nothing. Silence reigns while he takes his place at the front of the choir stalls and waits as we file in to our places. And then, at last, we're ready to sing the way the choirmaster wants.'

The girls were quiet for a few moments, and then Jo said: 'So what are you doing with your life now then?'

Before he could answer, Ruby looked at her watch:

'Oh my God! Look at the time. Gran will have been waiting ages for us. We've got to get going. Remember we said we would meet her at the bookshop by four fifteen and it's nearly that now!'

The girls stood up, scrambling to pick up their things, apologising to Stuart for rushing off.

'No sweat,' he said. 'Hey, Jo, why don't I give you my number? You can give me a call if you think I can help with your band. I'm a good guitarist you know.'

'Great,' said Jo. She could tell that Emily was jealous that Stuart seemed to have picked her to exchange numbers with, and she couldn't help feeling pleased. She rummaged in her bag and pockets for her phone. No sign of it!

'I can't find my phone,' she blurted out, beginning to panic. How in the world could it have gone missing? Her first thought was how furious her mother would be if she had lost it, and her second was that Stuart would think she was useless.

'I know I had it in the Pitt Rivers, I sent a text to Dad.'

Emily and Ruby stared at Jo, unable to help. There was nothing for it – Jo would have to go back, re-trace her steps to see if she had left it on the bench where they'd all been sitting making notes. The three of them agreed that Emily and Ruby would go on ahead to keep the appointment with Ruby's gran, and that Emily would swap numbers with Stuart. Jo watched helplessly as Emily slipped her phone out of her bag and started to key in Stuart's number.

She hurried out of the covered market alone. After the cosy warmth of the café, the company of her friends and the sweet taste of hot chocolate, the cold air of winter hit her full in the face.

As she rushed through the busy streets back to Oxford's renowned natural history museum, a faint image of a strange girl started forming in her mind. She had wondered, at the time, if the girl might have been following them. She was beginning to get a gut feeling that it was when that girl was around that she had lost her phone. It was getting very near to closing time, so clutching her bag, she broke into a run.

CHAPTER 3

Closing Time

Jo stepped into the vast, now nearly empty main court of the Oxford University Museum of National History. She hesitated. She was startled to find that the Victorian Gothic building, so enticingly atmospheric when bustling with daytime visitors, was ever so slightly creepy when nearly deserted. Outside, the dark of the late afternoon seemed to have wrapped itself around the building and now Jo almost regretted the kindness of the museum's staff in letting her in for a last minute search for her lost mobile phone. Only a few visitors remained, hanging back, reluctant to leave, and one by one, lights were being switched off: a deliberate signal to the stragglers to hurry up and head home.

The exhibits ranged from towering dinosaurs to smaller wildlife specimens, beavers, otters, fierce-eyed polecats in illuminated cases, and as Jo walked tentatively past them, she imagined that they had been waiting for this moment to claim the building back from the humans, just like in the movie that her brother loved so much – 'A Night at the Museum'.

It was so quiet, Jo could hear her own footsteps echoing softly but insistently on the wide expanse of shiny floor. She became aware of another person's footsteps behind her, keeping almost exact time with hers. She turned round to face her shadower and there she was – the strange girl who Jo had sensed rather than seen when she had been in the museum earlier in the day. The girl had long black hair and enigmatic eyes – eyes that seemed to change colour from brown to green and back again to brown. And somewhere at the back of Jo's mind, she was aware that her fear was being calmed by the distant sound of drums – a fascinating blend of rhythms that managed to both intensify and lull her senses at the same time. Through her confusion she was certain of at least one thing: in all her years as a drummer, attending different workshops and classes, she had never experienced rhythms like these. Yes – 'experienced' was the right word, Jo thought to herself. The word 'heard' wouldn't really do justice to the sounds that throbbed in her head.

'I'm Mela,' the girl said suddenly, her voice somehow managing to stop the sound of the drums. 'I hope you enjoyed that? I wanted to share my music with you. You're an amazing drummer, aren't you? I'm jealous of that – I've never been able, that is allowed, to play the drums.'

'Sometimes I think that my parents wish they had not allowed *me* to play the drums,' said Jo, amazed that she was saying such a thing to this total stranger, this girl who said her name was Mela.

They had drawn alongside one of the museum's most celebrated treasures – the *Raphus Cucullatus* – the mummified head and foot of a dodo – the flightless bird that European sailors had first encountered on the Indian Ocean island of Mauritius in 1598. Jo noticed how she was thinking about the exhibit at the same time as listening to the girl – as if the stranger enabled her brain to do several things at the same time. And she wasn't scared or even surprised about this.

'Who are you Mela?' asked Jo. 'Come clean. You were following me earlier too, weren't you? Should I be freaking out?'

Mela laughed. 'I know you're not frightened of me, Jo.'

'So you know my name too.' Jo said. 'Somehow *that* doesn't freak me out either. But I do feel a bit spooked looking at this poor extinct bird.'

And then Jo realised why she wasn't afraid of Mela and what seemed like her ability to read minds.

The strange girl felt like an old friend even though Jo had only just met her. She felt relaxed and happy in her company – and glad that she wasn't in that vast main court of the deserted museum by herself.

'It's not spooky,' said Mela, placing her hand on the dodo's exhibition case. 'Just sad. I hate to think of them being driven to extinction through hunting and predators and the destruction of their natural habitat.'

Jo found herself looking closely at Mela's hand on the case. It was a slim, light brown hand, ordinary in every way except that it had seven digits instead of five. How could that be? Nobody had seven digits!

The surprised words came out of her mouth before she could stop them: 'You've got six fingers and a thumb! Mela, how come?'

Then Jo hoped that she hadn't sounded rude. Mela's hand didn't look deformed, but what if she had hurt her new friend's feelings?

'Don't worry, Jo' Mela reassured her. 'Most people from my time – the future – have hands like this. We have the alteration at birth.'

'It's not genetic then?' asked Jo. She realised that she had accepted Mela's extraordinary explanation completely, without questioning it; that the girl came from another time – not the past, but the future.

'No it's not genetic. It's just useful and I suppose, perhaps, a sort of fashion thing.'

Jo found herself somehow linking in her mind the strangeness of standing in front of all that was left of an extinct species – the museum's priceless specimen. And at the same time being in conversation with a girl who had somehow managed to visit the twenty-first century, from a future time, one that she couldn't possibly imagine. Her first thought was that these two things fitted together perfectly – two halves of a mystery that coming together solved everything. Her second thought was that while her friends would never believe her if she told them, she instinctively knew that her academic parents with their thirst for knowledge, above all else, would be beside themselves with excitement. Jo suddenly felt proud and privileged. It was she and not they that had some part to play in Mela's story.

'Why me, Mela?' Jo asked.

'Because you are quite special.' Mela said this very simply. Jo said nothing, a little embarrassed and even bewildered – earlier that day she had not been feeling special at all, she'd been feeling quite the opposite. Then she remembered why she had come back to the museum.

'And when can I have my mobile back?' She was absolutely sure that Mela had taken her phone for some strange reason of her own.

'Sorry about that, Jo,' Mela replied, handing Jo's mobile back to her. 'We borrowed it. I've got quite a bit of explaining to do now and not very much time to do it in. Is that OK.'

'Fine, I'm listening.'

'First off, on your mobile you've now got three extra buttons on the right-hand side.' Jo looked and saw that there were three buttons that had not been on the phone previously – one black, a green and a red.

Mela pointed to the black button. 'That button is for information. When you get home, find somewhere where you can be alone and then press it. You'll be told all about the Scientific History and Art Reclamation Programme, but remember you must find somewhere where you will not be interrupted by anyone else. After listening to the whole explanation, you will be invited to be on a time travel programme. Your proposed programme is number 15800. Your participation will help us to piece together more of humankind's history. We've already been finding out about our history from time travel exploration. But your century is our limit. That's why we need you to go back further for us and gather information. A few young people of about your age have already helped us.'

'I get it' said Jo, looking back again at the dodo in the glass case. She pointed at the information about the bird that was on display. 'It says here that these remains contain '*the only surviving soft tissue from the bird, and scientists have been able to extract the DNA fragments that have thrown new light on the bird's evolution.*' So I'm guessing people from your time are working in a similar way?'

'That is very clever of you to draw that parallel, Jo.' Mela smiled. 'I wish I had more time to explain it to you. But don't worry, you'll be learning as you go along. Like me in a way. You see, I'm an advanced student of SHARP, that's short for the Scientific History and Art Reclamation Programme. There's another student called Kazaresh, and his contact from your time has already made a few trips back in time.'

Jo's eyes widened. 'And your other contacts in my time? How many people have you worked with already?'

'Only one. She's a musician like you, but she has a classical music background. She's an amazing violinist. My first degree was music too, so I feel comfortable with musicians. That's why I have chosen musicians. And I like it that you play drums in a band. So twenty-first century!'

'After hearing drums from your time, Mela, I'm starting to feel a bit like these dinosaurs on display! I'll never be able to play like that,' Jo laughed, but then noticed that Mela's expression was serious now.

'You do understand what I'm asking you to do, don't you Jo?' the girl asked her.

Jo found herself taking a deep breath and then uttering words which a mere half hour earlier would have sounded unimaginable, unbelievable, unreal:

'Yes. You're asking me...' Jo paused, wondering if she should pinch herself to make sure she wasn't dreaming, just as they always did in the stories.

'...You're asking me to *travel back in time*, like those other children you've mentioned.'

'Don't worry Jo,' Mela said, her voice surprisingly matter of fact. 'They've all come back safely.'

'Well thank goodness for that!' Jo exclaimed and they both laughed. In the distance, a member of the museum staff was gesturing to them to leave. Jo realised with a shock that they were now the only visitors left.

'I knew we'd have to hurry this, Jo.' Mela said. 'I needed a bit longer to talk about that background to

SHARP, but remember the black button will tell you everything else you need to know.'

They started to head quickly towards the entrance, past the towering figures of the dinosaur skeletons, now indistinct like giant lumps of rock in the dim light. Jo had been so engrossed with Mela that she had not noticed that nearly all of the lights in the main court had been turned off.

'One last question then Mela,' said Jo. And now it was her own expression that was serious. 'What went wrong? For the human race, I mean? Here we are with the dodo and the dinosaurs. They all died out. What went wrong for us that you're having to piece the past together again? Why doesn't your time have the records anymore?'

Jo would have described the expression on Mela's face at that moment as 'haunted' as her friend searched for the right words to answer Jo's question, and her enigmatic green-brown eyes seemed to turn to the colour of sadness.

'We almost lost everything in the Dark Chaos' Mela said. 'Most of the records, most of everything, really.... Then we had the start of New Democracy- no nationalities anymore, just humankind. We're piecing it back together with time travel. But, as I said, your century's our limit. That's why we have to ask you to go further back for us.'

Jo had been hurrying, concerned that they had stretched the museum staff's patience to the limit, and her friend's voice was starting to fade out, as if she was leaving her behind. She turned towards her new friend to make sure she was keeping up, but Mela was now as dim a figure as the dinosaurs in the darkness: not moving, yet somehow further away. Was it just another trick of the light, or was Mela fading? Becoming indistinct? Was everything Jo had just experienced simply a weird trick that her own mind had played on her, unnerved as she had been by the atmosphere in the darkening building? But there was the new black button on her mobile and two other buttons that hadn't been there before either. As Jo stepped outside, back onto the busy streets of the city, she knew in her heart that Mela had been real.

CHAPTER 4

A Full Explanation Of The Scientific History And Arts Reclamation Programme

Ruby called her gran a 'soft touch' and she was. Even though Jo had kept her and the other two girls waiting ages outside the bookshop, she smiled indulgently at Jo as she hurried to join them.

'I am sorry, so sorry for keeping you waiting,' Jo gasped.

'Never mind, dear. Did you find your mobile?'

'Was it there?' asked Ruby and Emily almost together. They were all looking at her expectantly.

'Yes! It was handed in…' Jo knew she needed to lie. '…but I had to wait quite a while for the receptionist, who had logged it, because she was away in another part of the building, that's why I took so long getting here.' Jo was stunned at how easy she found it to make up a false story.

'You were so lucky someone handed it in!' Emily exclaimed. ' My mother would kill me if I lost my mobile.'

'I think that might be a little bit of an exaggeration, Emily,' said Ruby's gran gently. 'Now I must get all you girls home. Come on let's find the car.'

Now that they were in their first term of Year 8, the three girls were allowed some independence by their respective parents, but usually only with a parent or grandparent out in the city as well. That person was designated the adult 'in charge' for the day – the families took the responsibility in turn.

On the short drive back to the district where they all lived, Jo switched on her newly-returned mobile and found a long, irritable voice-mail message from her mother. Ruby's gran had been obliged to text her telling her why Jo had not yet joined them. Her mother's annoyed tones warned Jo that she would be grounded unless she kept to 'the rules': no freedom from now on unless she kept her mobile with her at all times, charged up, in credit and switched on! Even more important: Jo must *not* be late to the rendezvous with the grown-up in charge unless she had a really good reason.

'Boring, boring, boring' thought Jo, as she listened. She hoped that her mother would still be out collecting Ollie from the Sunday Choral Evensong at Magdalen College when she got home. If her dad was in his study, she might even be able to escape to the privacy of her own room before her brother got back. Then she would be able to press the new black button on her mobile. Who knew what incredible information it might reveal about the possible opportunity for her to time travel? Time travel! Jo couldn't help smiling to herself as she considered what her mother's reaction might be when she returned from another century, let alone half an hour late from the Natural History Museum!

Luck was on Jo's side when she let herself into her home with the set of house keys that her parents had recently entrusted her with. Her father barked out a genial 'hello Jo' from behind the closed door of his study as he heard her coming in, but otherwise the house was quiet and empty. He'd stay immersed in his books for the time being, she guessed rightly. Craving a sugar rush to give her confidence for her date with destiny, Jo helped herself to a cloudy lemonade from the fridge and picked off a chocolate in the shape of a bell from the Christmas tree in the living room. She felt a bit guilty about consuming so much sugar in one day, but then, this was no ordinary day, and she needed to psyche herself up to pressing that button on her mobile.

She went up to her bedroom and sat herself down on her favourite seat – the padded stool that was part of her drum kit – and took out her mobile, confident there would be no interruptions. She took a deep breath and pressed the black button.

She watched intently as the screen slid away from the base of her mobile and expanded. 'How do they do that?' she wondered aloud. No sound came from the phone, but now the screen was expanding to about the size of a 24 inch TV screen and hovering a few feet in front of her, its edges defined by a shiny black rim. Jo gasped as a message appeared in black letters on a background of swirling colours:

‹WELCOME JO TO SHARP 15800›

You can put the mobile down now. The screen will stay in place until you press the black button again.

Jo immediately obeyed the instruction and put the phone down. The message was fading now, but a background of intense swirling colours had taken its place, seeming to spin off the screen into the air around her. Then the screen cleared for a moment and a new message appeared:

After you have read all the following, think about what we are asking you to do. All the instructions and communications after this come to you from Mela, a fully-endorsed student of the University belonging to SHARP. Mela's tutor, Professor Aurelia Dobbs, is overseeing all of the programme and could possibly contact you as well.

This is an invitation to you to join our project. Thank you for taking the time to find out about us, and if you decide not to accept our invitation, we apologise for any inconvenience to you that might have been caused by the changes to your mobile phone. We will return it to its original state. We have contacted you because we think you are particularly suited to project 15800 but we will quite understand if you decline to take part. Your safety is of the utmost importance to us and in almost all respects we can guarantee that you can travel backwards in time and return to your home time zone without any ill effects whatsoever or any danger to yourself or the people you meet on your travels. However, every activity in life can result in danger, as I am sure you are aware, and so we cannot guarantee ultimate safety.

As soon as Jo finished reading, the screen faded and the next message appeared.

We repeat: After you have read all the following, think about what we are asking you to do. Finally, we want you to know that your involvement with this project is very helpful to us, the remaining humankind of the world, and that, although it will be impossible for you to understand why, you will be making a contribution to the continuance of civilisation upon earth.
Our Company Policy is: Be of good hope and travel back in time and return in the spirit of greater good for all mankind.

The screen changed once more. This time there was a countdown with numbers flashing past the screen so quickly it was impossible to read them until they began to slow, and then Jo realised it was a countdown of years. At 2010 the numbers halted and the following words appeared on the screen:

‹INSTRUCTIONS to Jo Kelly from Mela Wang›

Hello Jo. It was great meeting you at the museum. The instructions below come from me but they are standard SHARP instructions. At the end, you can ask questions by sending a text to SHARP 15800.

‹Pre-Travel Information›

When there is the possibility of a journey to a different time zone, the screen of your mobile will glow blue and you will feel a low-level vibration, different in pulse to its usual one. This may last for up to two hours your time. After that, the opportunity will have passed, but you will be sent a further opportunity.

‹Travel Information›

If you are ready to travel, make sure you are alone and somewhere where you will not be interrupted. You will be gone for between ten and fifteen minutes, your time. It will seem to you, when you are on a time journey, that you are away for much longer. It is not desirable for anyone to see you go or return. So make sure that no one is likely to be worried by your disappearance.

Wearing clothes is not helpful so you will need to wear something skin-tight — what you call a swimming costume is best. You will have received from us a small bag that you must wear. It doesn't need ties or anything. It is called a time/space bag. When you have taken your clothes off, press the bag to your waist, on top of any skin-tight item you are wearing. Do this BE-FORE you press the green button on your mobile to go. I repeat: the green button for 'go'. The time/space bag contains a small silver disc that you must put on your forehead when you arrive. The disc is almost weightless so you will not notice it, but it will record everything you see. It only activates when it is worn, and it only lasts a short while, so do not put it on until AFTER you arrive in the past. On your arrival, take the disc out and press it to your forehead. The backing disc will come away. Put this and your phone into the bag and secure the fastening. You'll find that the bag attaches itself to you without any discomfort. It cannot be taken from you and assures your safe return. I was wearing one in the museum when we talked.

‹Journey›

When you are ready to go, key in the project number 15800 and press the **black** button. A screen will appear that will tell you where you are going, what you will see and who you will meet. It identifies a Destination. Read these travel instructions very carefully and when you are sure you have understood them, key in the project number 15800 and then press the **green** button. The system will be activated and you will be transported to the time zone indicated. Near to where you arrive, there will be a pile of clothes suitable for the time and place. You must put these on as quickly as possible.

The people you meet will either mistake you for someone they know or will not be surprised that a stranger is amongst them. On your journeys you will find that you can help people, this you should do. Never do anything unkind. This is very important.

‹Return Journey›

The **red** button on your phone facilitates your return. When it is time for you to return, you will feel the phone vibrating very distinctly. You will have to take off the clothes and leave them in a pile, preferably somewhere they cannot be seen too easily. Take the phone out of the time/space bag, key in 15800 and press the **red** button. If you need to return because of danger before the phone vibrates, key in 15800, remove the clothes as described above and press the red button. This should only be done under real emergency conditions.

<After your visit>

We will contact you after your visit to give you an assessment of how well you have done .

We will be sending you an option for travel in the next few days. If you do not take up the option for this or the next two opportunities, we will assume that you have decided to decline our invitation and we will return your mobile to its original state and retrieve our travel bag.

At last the screen cleared and the words 'Goodbye for now' appeared. Then the floating screen immediately shrank back to fit its normal space on the mobile. Jo switched the phone off. Excitement and a mass of other feelings were colliding about inside her, zooming off in as random a way as protons and neutrons inside an atom. She wanted to burst into her father's study and shout out: 'I'm going to be a time traveller'. But she knew she couldn't do that.

In order to calm down, she went over to her desk and started to write down as much as she could remember of the instructions she had just been sent. Never very good with numbers, she wrote 15800 several times across the top of the page in her notebook. She was just beginning to feel unbearably restless when she heard the door opening downstairs as her mother and brother returned from Magdalen College: their timing was perfect. Forgetting her mother's grumpy text, she ran down the stairs to meet them, smiling a real welcome home.

'Have you had a good evening, Ollie?' she asked.

CHAPTER 5

Staircase 3, Room 3

Jo struggled to concentrate at school the next day, even though she thought it unlikely that the SHARP people would contact her there. For one thing, school rules meant mobile phones had to be switched off during the day, but of course, they could probably get round such a matter. She found herself constantly taking her mobile out of her pocket and running her fingers over the three extra buttons and going over and over her meeting with Mela at the museum.

Try as she might to listen to the teachers, intense nervous excitement prevented her from paying any real attention. She wondered what period of history they would send her back to, and she wished she'd listened more to her father who was a passionate historian. She'd always disappointed him with low marks in history: how odd it was that she, of all people, should have been chosen to travel back into the past. Why hadn't she paid more attention in history lessons? She could kick herself now.

Monday was the day her father met her after

school at Blackwell's, the bookshop in town – a routine they'd shared for years. As she made her way to the shop, she thought of how she would try belatedly to get some ideas from her father.

'What makes a person a good historian, Dad?' Jo asked him, as they browsed together among the book-shelves. Matthew put down the book he was turning over in his hands and tried not to show his surprise: this was not the kind of question Jo usually asked him.

'Enthusiasm for the subject's the most important thing,' he answered, '…more important than depth of knowledge or expertise or any of those things. That's why any child can become a good historian if they have enthusiasm.'

Jo smiled. This was encouraging news. 'Go on.' she pressed. 'What else?'

'Well – I suppose it's knowing where and how to look for the right information – how to find the details, and it's always the details, that tell the story. You might need to look in the most unexpected places.'

'Like where?' Jo said, puzzled.

'Take this book, for example,' Matthew picked out a random book from the shelf in front of them: *Oxford Trees* by Sophie Huxley. 'Who'd have thought that trees could play such an important part in our city's literary history, warranting an academic work such as this?' Matthew flicked through the pages as he carried on talking, warming to his subject. 'The ancient chestnut tree in the Lamb and Flag passage turns up in Dorothy L. Sayers book, *Gaudy Night*. Or what about that strange tree at Christ Church, the Pococke plane? That's supposed to have been the inspiration for Lewis Carroll's Jabberwock. You see where I'm going with this? Everything has its own story to tell about the past – even trees.'

As they left the shop, Jo asked for more information. 'And what if you were looking through say, historical documents? How do you pick out the right ones?'

Matthew smiled and gave his daughter an affectionate hug. 'This is *my* Jo Kelly, isn't it? I did meet the right daughter in Blackwell's, didn't I?' he laughed.

'People change, Dad,' Jo answered. 'I'm going to listen to you more from now on.'

'Goodness! What an honour' Matthew said, teasing her just a little, though he tried not to smile again at Jo's earnest expression. He certainly didn't want to put her off her new found interest in history.

'Well – I can give you one good example off the top of my head' Matthew continued, thinking about how best to answer her latest question. 'When our own Robin Darwall-Smith – you know – the archivist for Magdalen College? Well, when he was researching the Oxford University's history, he said that it was often the papers that might look terribly dull at first, that would then reveal the most extraordinary things. For example, back in 1600, students used to give their tutors money, which the tutors then spent on the students' behalf. So he said it was the account books belonging to the tutors from that time that wrote a large chunk of his University College history book for him: from those he found out what books people were buying, what clothes they were wearing, what they bought to decorate their rooms... all of that helped him to understand what it was like being a student at a University 400 years ago.'

As they walked home together Jo, listening intently to her father's explanations, felt incredibly happy. At last she felt like his equal. She was going to be a seeker after knowledge, as well. She longed to be able to share her news with him, but remembered that Mela and SHARP had instructed her not to talk to anyone about their contact. All she knew was that at any minute now she might get the call to time travel, so she had to make use of her father's wisdom while she could. 'And another example,' her father continued. He was talking non-stop now that she'd got him started on one of his favourite subjects. 'Just look at those gargoyles round the side of the Bodleian Library.' He pointed upwards to the strange figures protruding from the top of the wall of the building they were just passing. 'All those new ones on the north-west side…' he gestured to the nine new faces amongst the more ancient of the stone grotesques. '…think how the stonemasons who built the new gargoyles must have researched past techniques and used their craft to tell our city's history! Do you remember who gave them the designs?' her father asked.

Jo did remember. 'Yes, of course, Dad' she replied. 'The University ran a competition inviting school kids in the area to design a gargoyle with a connection to local history.'

'Because one of the existing rows of the gargoyles on the library had completely eroded,' her father carried on. 'Do you remember? And I wanted you to enter and you didn't?'

Jo looked sheepish. 'Couldn't be bothered at the time,' she confessed. 'But I would now.'

'I should hope so!'

'That one's my favourite, Dad' Jo said, pointing

at the image of the C. S. Lewis character, Aslan the Lion. 'I think he looks well cool as a stone lion!'

'Yes, I agree he works really well as a gargoyle,' Matthew replied. 'My favourite's the Thomas Bodley one though – with his twirly moustache and stone beard!'

'But look at Aslan's stoney whiskers!!' argued Jo. 'Beat those!'

'I admit – they are hard to beat' Matthew laughed. 'But my point is, Jo, that history is every-where. It's all around us. Every tree, every stone, every dull entry in an old account book has its story to tell. You just need to look carefully.'

As they arrived home, Jo promised her father that from now on she would be looking. It wasn't long, though, before their companionable, contemplative mood was interrupted. Oliver opened the door as he heard them coming, fired up with some new excite-ment.

'Grandma's Christmas calendar's arrived!' he shouted. 'Do you think there might be chocolates in it this time?' he added, hopefully.

'You know she doesn't send those kinds of ad-vent calendars, Ollie,' Jo corrected him. 'It'll be a mag-ical Christmas scene from long ago. Stars sparkling over snow covered rooftops, maybe? Or smiling children in Victorian clothes untying the ribbons on their pressies?'

Oliver tried hard to hide his disappointment at the thought of no chocolates, and Jo was already looking at him disdainfully. 'I bet I know what you want' she said. 'A chocolate spectacular with a superhero on the front. Or maybe Dr. Who or Spongebob.'

Oliver was hurt by Jo's tone of voice and tried to hide it by ripping the envelope as he pulled out the calendar. Matthew and Harriet had gathered round, ready to be part of the ritual.

'Careful, Oliver,' Harriet warned him. 'You might tear the picture.'

'Why are little brothers so annoying?' Jo needled him.

'Steady on Jo' Matthew said. 'Don't spoil things.'

'Sorry, Dad' Jo said, anxious not to ruin her new solidarity with her father, as an old-fashioned Christmas scene did indeed emerge intact from the large envelope. Jo realised that it didn't matter that she was nearly thirteen. She still loved advent calendars and stockings and decorated trees. She didn't think she'd ever grow out of them.

'It *is* perfect' Oliver stated. 'Just that it would be

even more perfect if there was a chocolate behind every window! But before you remind me – yes, I do know I can't eat them before a service and I do know that Grandma thinks all children now are spoilt and have too many treats and too many toys.'

'She's never forgotten the war,' Harriet said. 'She was only four when World War 2 started. Can you imagine Christmas with rationing and blackouts?'

'We know, we know.' Oliver chimed in. 'She's told us all about the families saving up their weekly coupons for butter and sugar... if they were lucky.'

'And doing without meat and treats and fruit and stuff,' Jo added.

'And how she had a diet of porridge and chips and toast,' Oliver continued.

Matthew laughed. 'Well! I can see she's made her point!'

It was as they were opening the first window of their new calendar that Jo felt her phone inside her pocket vibrating with a quick staccato pulse it had never had before.

Oh my God – she thought to herself. This must be it! The call to time travel.

Jo excused herself and went upstairs to her bedroom, citing urgent homework as her reason for leaving the cosy family scene. Harriet and Matthew exchanged glances but let her go without saying anything: Jo wasn't normally known for her conscientious attitude towards her homework. Things were looking up.

As she closed the door to her room behind her, Jo noticed that there – as SHARP had promised – was the small, flat brown bag that they had said they would send. It was in her favourite spot, sitting on the stool that was part of her drum kit, just so that she wouldn't miss it. And even more exciting: as she flicked open her mobile phone, the screen went a vivid blue. She quickly keyed in 15800 and pressed the black button, watching the screen enlarge to about the size of an exercise book.

The message read:

Welcome Jo. We hope you will decide to travel with SHARP. If you decide to go, press the green button. Here are the details of your current travel option.

‹Time Zone›
December 1939

‹Place›

Magdalen College, Oxford

‹Landing›
New Buildings, Staircase 3, Room 3, Inside wardrobe

‹Instructions›
Stay put; let yourself be found

‹Conditions›
It is almost four months after the announcement that Britain is at war with Germany. World War 2 shows no sign of ending quickly, as some people have expected. Weather — wintry. Threat level — mild to moderate: caution advised, though no bombing raids expected at this time. Mood — gloomy.

'What a coincidence!' Jo thought. 'We were just talking about Grandma and the war, and now I'm going back to that time…'

She carried on reading SHARP's message:

‹Equipment›
Mobile phone, travel bag. Mobile phone fitted with beam of light, activated when t-o-r-c-h is keyed in (only use sparingly).

If you wish to travel do as follows:

> Wear swimming costume for time travel journey
> Press the time/space travel bag close to your body so that it is attached
> Key in 15800 on your mobile
> Press the green button.

Have a good trip.

'Simple!' Jo said out loud. 'Or not – depending on how you look at it. They make it sound so easy.' She was shivering slightly with excitement, then said in a very calm voice: 'Well – we'll see. Here goes!'

Jo changed into her swimming costume, as instructed, and pressed the travel bag close to her body, so that it stuck there as if glued. Then, never one to turn down any kind of challenge, she keyed in 15800 and pressed the green button. At the back of her mind, she knew that Staircase 3, Room 3 in the New Buildings of Magdalen College held some significance, but in the excitement of the moment, this significance eluded her. She heard a faint, high-pitched whine, far off but coming nearer and nearer until it filled her whole head and then… Nothing.

CHAPTER 6

The Inklings

Jo barely noticed any sensation connected with the actual moment of time travel. Her eyes were tight shut. Before she dared to open them, she was aware that she felt extremely cold and uncomfortable. She was sitting with her body hunched up in a ball in a dark, cramped space that she assumed must be the wardrobe. Of all the places to land! Why a wardrobe? And dressed only in a swimming costume in the middle of winter! Jo shivered, but couldn't help smiling at the inappropriate nature of her dress for the season, and the indignation her mum would express if she knew.

This made her remember that there should be clothes for her somewhere around. She opened her eyes wide. Nothing. She could see nothing. The wardrobe door must be shut: she was engulfed by darkness. Darkness was all around and a strong smell – a strange, musty, slightly chemical smell. What was it? She had smelt it before but couldn't remember where. Somewhere, not too far off, was the sound of voices murmuring, and laughter.

There was nothing for it – although SHARP had said she must only use the torch sparingly, she would have to activate it or she'd never get anywhere. The mobile was glowing with a soft blue from the screen so she could just see to key in t-o-r-c-h. Soon a thin beam illuminated her surroundings.

The wardrobe she had landed in evidently belonged to a man: hanging up were pairs of baggy, grey flannel trousers, tweed jackets, underwear in the form of woollen vests and braces, some sleeveless woollen pullovers and two coats. Everything was very neatly ordered. Jo half-expected to find the clothes for her on the hangers but there was nothing for a girl. She noticed that to one side of the wardrobe, hanging together, there was academic dress – a dark suit and white shirt, a mortar board and a long black scholar's gown. Jo was familiar with this kind of clothing as worn by the Oxford University students or their tutors, the dons. Her father was still wearing almost identical dress to formal functions in 2010.

She then flashed the torch around the floor of the wardrobe, wondering if her clothes would be waiting for her there. Sure enough, there was a tiny bundle of girls' clothes: a plain, blue dress, old-fashioned in its simplicity of style, a pair of white girls' socks – she hadn't worn white socks for years, a peculiar yellow woollen cardigan and a pair of flat black shoes with a single strap that looked a bit like ballet pumps. Two blue ribbons for her hair were at the bottom of the pile. Jo dressed quickly, quite a feat in her cramped surroundings. Then she tied her hair up into bunches with the ribbons, smiling to herself as she thought about how Emily and Ruby would tease her mercilessly if they could see her. This look was a million miles away from her usual jeans and cool t-shirts! In spite of her new outfit, Jo still felt cold and the awful smell was becoming unbearable. Suddenly, she knew what it was. Mothballs! Grandma had them in her wardrobe – that's where she had met the smell before. They were on the floor of the wardrobe and crunched under her feet like frosted snow as she tried to move around. How annoying that she couldn't go anywhere – SHARP had made it clear she would have to stay put until found. She would just have to be patient.

She sat down again, feeling the hard, smooth wood of the wardrobe against her back. She switched the torch off and was just about to return her mobile to the bag, which was now under her dress, when she re-membered the disc that she had to put on her forehead. She took the disc from the bag and pressed it tightly to her forehead. Just as SHARP had described, the backing came away and the film seemed to dissolve into her skin. Weird.

She felt badly cramped now, with no way of knowing how long she'd have to stay like this. She realised that she felt faintly sick and slightly dizzy – was it the shock of time travel? She decided to concentrate on the sound of the voices she could hear close by and the laughter that rang out at regular intervals, reassuring her that at least the group she might soon be joining was having a very merry evening.

At first, Jo couldn't make out much of what the voices were saying, though she could hear that all the people talking and laughing were men. Gradually, her ears became accustomed to having to work harder and her eyes began to adjust to the lack of light inside the wardrobe. The men seemed to be reciting verse to each other and one voice had a particularly sonorous quality that resonated around her, as though the wardrobe acted as a chamber of echoes whenever this particular person spoke:

'*Hwaet!*' the voice commanded. 'Listen,my good friends! The shortest day of the year will soon be upon us. In honour of the occasion, I've chosen to recite one of John Donne's finest poems, the *Nocturnal Upon St.Lucy's Day*. I know Donne is not entirely to your taste, Jack, but I trust you will indulge me.'

'Proceed, Tollers!' another voice replied. 'The shortest day, the longest night. How appropriate a metaphor for this infernal war we're having to endure!'

Jo couldn't help thinking that the men were in re-markably good spirits considering that World War 2 was now a shadow hanging over all their lives. And SHARP had mentioned a mood of 'gloom'. Not here!

'But let us not forget', the second voice continued, 'that war or no war – we still have these convivial times together when our feet are spread out towards the blaze and our drinks at our elbows; when the whole world, and something beyond the world, opens itself to us and our shared thoughts.'

'Well said, Jack!' the first voice agreed. 'But, now I beg for a solemn and respectful silence – appropriate for the mood of this poem.'

The man cleared his throat and began:

Tis the year's midnight, and it is the day's,
Lucy's, who scarce seven hours herself unmasks,
The sun is spent, and now his flasks
send forth light squibs, no constant rays;
The world's whole sap is sunk...

At this moment, Jo couldn't help sneezing loudly, several times, completely spoiling the mood that the person reciting the poem was trying to create. The mothballs were finally proving too much for her.

There was an unexpected break in the reading of the poem, as the men realised that they had an intruder in their midst. Jo braced herself, waiting to be found. She began to feel very nervous – were these men going to be cross?

The man who opened the door of the wardrobe and looked in at Jo was a big man, probably in his early forties, she thought. He was solidly built and had a rather red complexion, strong features and fine, expressive eyes. Much to her relief, he smiled at her immediately, seeming delighted to see her and not at all surprised to find a twelve-year-old girl hiding in his wardrobe.

As the light filtered in, Jo blinked, stood up and stepped out of the wardrobe at last. She could now see that her wardrobe was in this man's bedroom and that it was in his study beyond this room that the man's friends were gathered around the fire. So that was why the voices had sounded muffled and distant until her ears had adjusted.

'Well, well!' the man exclaimed. 'I do believe you

must be one of our evacuees! Playing hide and seek no doubt. And my guess is you've been successfully evading your potential captors all evening. Not a single child has come looking for you my dear. No one has discovered your hiding place – until now, of course.'

Jo smiled at this kindly man, introduced herself by name and held out her hand politely for him to shake.

'So – you're Josephine, are you? Jo for short? Glad to make your acquaintance. I'm Clive Staples Lewis. But no one calls me Clive - just as no one calls you Josephine, eh? All my friends call me Jack.'

Suddenly, Jo remembered the significance of Staircase 3, Room 3 in the New Buildings of Magdalen College. How could she have forgotten? These had been the rooms of the world famous writer, C.S.Lewis, whose Narnia books she had loved reading when she was younger. And now here he was in person. That meant that she must have landed slap bang in the middle of a meeting of Lewis and his literary friends! The man she had heard referred to as 'Tollers' must be the writer of *The Lord of the Rings Trilogy*, J.R.R. Tolkien! Her parents would have given anything to have been present at a meeting of these men!

'But my dear girl! You're shivering! Come in and

warm yourself by our fire before you catch your death!'

'Thank you…er, Jack,' Jo replied as politely as she could, though not yet quite sure how people of her age were supposed to address grown-ups in the 1930's. She guessed that she would have to appear more formal in her manner than was normal for her in her own time.

As she was leaving the cold bedroom for the warmth of the study, she took a quick look round, surprised at how modest it was. Besides her wardrobe, there was an iron bedstead and a wash-stand with a hole in the top that held a china basin, in which there stood a jug full of water. Under the washstand was a large, enamel bucket. Beside the bed, there was a brown chair and laid out on top of the bed, a camel hair dressing gown and flannel pyjamas. Jo guessed that Jack, as she strangely now thought of him, rather than the famous name of C.S.Lewis, rarely if ever slept in college: the pyjamas looked too perfectly folded and unused. Of course, he would have a real home somewhere, just as her own parents did, though they too had rooms in their colleges. She couldn't see out of Jack's bedroom as the brownish curtains were backed by the black ones required for the black-outs of the war years.

Jo remembered the camera on her forehead. She knew it should be recording events for SHARP and was anxious that it would send them a good, strong clear picture: attending a meeting of these famous persons, as she was about to do, would provide valuable and rare material for their Arts Reclamation Programme. Instinctively, she ran a hand across her forehead. It felt perfectly smooth and it was hard to believe that something in her skin was taking pictures! How much more sophisticated the technology of the future was: the travel bag into which she had put her mobile and the outer case of the disc, was now hugging the side of her body as though stuck there with super glue. She couldn't feel it at all, even with the weight of the phone in it. How neat! Well – she had obeyed SHARP's instructions to the letter, she could do nothing more.

'Welcome Jo – Daughter of Eve! Child from the Land of Wardrobe; welcome to our humble meeting of the Inklings!' C.S.Lewis introduced her with a flourish to the assembled men, all of similar age to himself.

As soon as he said the words 'the Inklings', Jo remembered her parents using this name. The Inklings had passed into Oxford history. She still felt cold and she edged towards the roaring fire in the grate, besides which was placed a large scuttle of coal. She couldn't help reaching her frozen hands out towards the flames.

'The college bedrooms are infernally cold,' said Lewis. 'Sometimes the sheets are so damp that steam rises when you get into bed! You chose the perfect hiding place, child, but with scant regard for your health! Sit down beside the fire and warm up here until your friends find you!'

Lewis then named the four other men present as Professor Tolkien, to be affectionately referred to as 'Tollers,' Lewis's brother Warren Lewis, otherwise known as 'Warnie', Charles Williams and Hugo Dyson: 'not a full-house of the Inklings, but five is a respectable turn-out!'

Jo sat down on the floor as close to the fire as she could, while Lewis placed himself next to Williams on the Chesterfield sofa. Warnie and Dyson sat smoking pipes in separate threadbare armchairs, their legs outstretched towards the fire, and Tollers, who had been reciting the poem, was still standing in front of the assembled company. He paused a moment to reach for an enamel beer jug on the table and refill everyone's tankard.

Then he looked at Jo with a twinkle in his eye.

'So – Jo, from the Land of Wardrobe. Did you come bearing your sandwiches and gas mask, like all the other evacuees?' Tolkien chuckled. 'What was in your very own special travel bag?'

Jo was taken aback. She felt as if Tolkien had rumbled her. How canny of him to mention her travel bag. By some strange means, did he know she was from the future? That she was not from the big cities that had sent all their children away to the countryside to help protect them from the bombing? He was a lighter and more graceful man than Lewis, with shining fair hair and shrewd but sensitive eyes that seemed to Jo to understand everything. For a brief moment, she was tempted to say how she had arrived there. To tell them the amazing truth. He would believe her, she knew that. But SHARP would not want that. Instinctively she knew they would be angry, perhaps very angry. So she summoned all her knowledge of Word War 2 evacuees that she had been taught in school, four years ago in Year 4. She looked Tolkien straight in the eyes:

'Yes, Professor Tolkien', she replied.

You may refer to me as Tollers in this company', he reminded her.

'Sorry. I mean Tollers,' Jo continued. 'I did come

bearing a bag of food for my day of travel, my gas mask - in a large cardboard box attached to a shoulder strap. And some spare clothes, toothbrush, comb, and a handkerchief. But at least I didn't bring head lice too – like some of my new friends!'

This got the laugh that Jo had hoped for, as she tried to divert Tolkien's attention from how she had got there.

'Some of the evacuees lodging in Christ Church were found not to have been baptised!' Warnie Lewis broke in. 'I hear this was hastily put right!'

'And did you enjoy what little of John Donne's poem I was able to recite, until you surprised us all with your sneezing?' Tolkien added.

'I expect it was the mothballs' Jack Lewis explained. 'I can't abide them either.'

Jo suddenly remembered the C.S.Lewis book that she had loved the most, *The Lion, the Witch and the Wardrobe*. How strange that she should have been found inside Lewis' wardrobe, and yet she was fairly sure that he had written this book after the war – long after this moment in his life that she was sharing now. She looked at Tolkien again and hugged her arms around her knees.

'Very much', she said, answering his question.

'But what did *Hwaet* mean?'

'Oh, Tollers always opens his recitals in the Early English style,' explained Hugo Dyson. 'It means *listen*! Though it sounds like *Quiet*! Perfect for silencing undergraduates!'

Jo was beginning to feel like an undergraduate herself and wondered if she should enter the spirit of the evening and contribute. At this moment, the perfect phrase popped into her head.

'You were saying that this war's like the longest night,' she said. 'To me the war feels as if it's always winter. Always winter and never Christmas.'

There was a moment's complete silence, as the profound sadness of Jo's observation struck all the men.

'How true', agreed Lewis. 'Always winter and never Christmas. I doubt if any of us scholars could have put it better ourselves. None of us will forget what you've said, Jo.'

Jo blushed, feeling a little like a fraud. It was of course, Lewis's own phrase she had used, not her own, though he could never have known this. Once again, she had the sense that Tolkien was observing her keenly, aware that she was not quite all that she was pretending to be. The others though were just sorry for her.

'Cheer up child!' Lewis boomed, jovial again. 'You must help us read tonight. On our bill of fare today we have a section of the new Hobbit book from Tollers, a nativity play from Charles and a chapter out of the book on the *Problem of Pain* from me. I think you would all agree that Jo will make a magnificent Mary in Charles's *The House By the Stable*. You are lucky child, that this nativity play is unusually intelligible for him!'

The assembled company laughed and Williams turned his bright, piercing eyes upon Jo.

'Yes – I'd be honoured if you'd play my Mary,' he agreed, throwing his cigarette into the grate and taking up a pile of extremely small, loose sheets from a cheap writing pad for memoranda. Jo fervently hoped that she'd be able to read his messy handwriting.

And so it was that for one night only, in December 1939, Jo became an honorary, though temporary, member of the Inklings in Lewis's study, Room 3, Staircase 3 of the New Buildings of Magdalen College. All thoughts of time and space vanished as she listened to all the men reading, sometimes joining in when invited, sometimes just absorbing the moment while the invisible film on her forehead recorded everything for others living in the world's distant future.

A few hours later, just as Jo was listening, mesmerised by the fire and by Tolkien's voice, to a newly reworked section of *The Fellowship of the Ring*, there was a loud knock on the door.

CHAPTER 7

Sparkle

C.S. Lewis opened the door of his study to find a college servant, a middle-aged woman wearing a cap and apron, standing at the door looking agitated. When the woman caught sight of Jo sitting by the fire, she immediately relaxed.

'Oh there you are, miss!' she burst out. 'We've been looking all over for you.' She turned to Lewis. 'Beg pardon, Sir,' she added, eager to explain her intrusion, which might otherwise have seemed too forward. Then, as now, Jo noticed the college 'scouts,' as the servants were called, were supposed to know their place.

'I've been sent from St. Hugh's to help out with the evacuees, Sir,' the woman continued. 'Magdalen's putting on an afternoon of Christmas merriment for the little ones, but it's taken us an age to find all the children after the hide and seek – what with the blackouts and all. Gets black as pitch round the college buildings at night when there's no moon. We've been all over!'

Jo quickly got to her feet, sorry to be leaving The Inklings, but anxious not to cause any trouble.

'Think nothing of it, my dear,' Lewis reassured the woman. 'Josephine has been safe here with us – and very well-behaved. But I'm sure she's eager to return to the festivities.'

'You can't be too careful what with this war on,' the scout continued. 'Only, funny things go on sometimes – I suppose it's not my place to mention them, being a servant.'

'So you work for St.Hugh's? They're turning your college into a military hospital, so I've heard,' Lewis observed.

'Yes, Sir. To specialise in treating head injuries,' she replied.

'Has that been a big adjustment for you scouts?' asked Lewis, politely.

The woman nodded her head. 'I used to wait upon the Hall and Senior Common Room. But I'm kitchen staff now. None of us know whether we're coming or going.'

'Good lord!' exclaimed Warnie Lewis from his armchair. 'Watch out or we'll all be over-run by civil servant chaps: it's a rum thing to watch bits of Balliol turning into the Foreign Office. And what do you think of poor old St. John's, controlling fish and potatoes for the Ministry of Food? They say it's the biggest fish and chip shop in the world! And that's not the half of it...'

The Inklings laughed, and bid Jo an affectionate farewell. She and the scout descended the steep wooden stairs down from Lewis's rooms together. Then they crossed the quad. It was almost dark already. Clouds scudded across the sky and the quarter moon was still pale in the last murmuring of daylight, so that Jo was glad to be able to follow the broad figure of the woman in front of her along the flagged pathway to the Junior Common Room. In some respects, Jo thought, Oxford colleges had changed little since the war. The names of things at least hadn't changed that much.

That late December afternoon, four women scouts were responsible for chaperoning the evacuee children and keeping them entertained. A few undergraduates still remained in the common room, huddled round the large coke brazier in the fireplace, lolling about in armchairs and reading the papers. They were wearing similar clothes to those worn by the Inklings – flannel trousers and tweed jackets – though most of them were also sporting extremely long woollen scarves in college colours, wound round their necks and dangling almost to their knees. Jo could understand why: even inside beside the fire, the bitter December chill seemed to penetrate the college buildings. Up on the walls, propaganda posters proclaimed their pointed festive messages. One had a picture of servicemen waving and underneath was written:

'DO YOUR DUTY! SEND US GREETING CARDS!'

Another read:

'GIVE WINGS TO YOUR THOUGHTS! SEND HIM A CHRISTMAS CARD'.

At the other end of the common room, gathered round large trestle tables were the evacuee children. They were leaving the undergraduates in peace, but otherwise they were a lively bunch. Jo watched the scouts trying to control them. Remembering what she had been doing at home on Saturday, she was amused to see that the scouts had provided lots of materials with which to make Christmas decorations. There was a great deal of cutting out and sticking going on with exclamations of:

'Please pass me the glue. I need it right now.'

'Can someone hold this for me for a moment?'

'Don't take all of the shiny paper – I want some!'

Although she would have liked to have joined this group of children of her own age, she noticed a boy of about seven who was sitting on his own at one end of the table. His sad face was keeping the other children away. Jo went and sat beside the boy in companionable silence. She sensed he wouldn't be ready to talk to her yet. After a while she got up and found a cardboard box, some paint and some scraps of material. She started to make a crib, and slowly the boy joined in.

'Oh that's nice,' said one of the scouts. 'You could make figures with pipe cleaners.'

Jo wondered what on earth these were and then realised, when the woman brought them to their table that they were the pieces of wire with coloured bits of wool attached that she had used one time in a primary school art project. She made Mary, and the boy made Joseph; they twisted the pipe cleaners into legs, arms and bodies. Then they added faces by painting on to cardboard circles and shredded wool to make the hair. The boy smiled at her several times but still didn't say anything in answer to her questions.

The other children had made long paper chains. When they started to try and hang them up, the undergraduates came over to help them reach the highest corners of the room. Then they moved onto games – musical chairs and pass the parcel. Her silent companion stayed away from the gaiety, preferring to carry on making things. Jo sensed that he was glad she had chosen to stay with him. She couldn't help wondering how Ollie would have coped with being sent away from home at that age, and she felt a pang of guilt as she remembered how grumpy she often was with him.

'What's your name?' she asked for about the third time as they sat side-by-side cutting out coloured paper in two different colours, and twisting the pieces together to make garlands.

'Philip,' he answered. 'You can call me Pip.'

'I'm Jo,' she replied. 'You look sad, Pip. Do you want to tell me what's wrong?'

'It's my toy monkey – Sparkle. My mum promised he'd look after me while I was away and brighten things up in the blackouts. But now he's lost and there's no one to look after me. And I'm scared of the dark without him.'

'Shall we look for him together?' Jo asked.

Pip brightened up immediately. 'Let's pull down that blackout curtain and pretend it's a magic carpet! We could go anywhere in the world to find him!'

'Even better – let's use this purple cloth as our magic carpet. It's all silky!' Jo said persuasively, keen to keep them out of trouble. 'Best not tear down the blackouts or the wardens will come looking for us.'

'But I hate the blackout curtains! I want to tear them *all* down!' argued Pip. 'You can't see anything anymore – no more shops lit up and they're all covered with anti-blast tape! I hate all this darkness! And now my Sparkle's gone too!'

Pip started to cry, but Jo quickly pulled out the purple cloth that covered the table they had been working on, hoping to distract him. Soon they were playing magic carpet make-believe games right up until the time the bell sounded for dinner in the hall. Jo hadn't had so much fun since she and Ollie had played like this when they were little.

The children ate tea in the huge dining hall with the dons and undergraduates, who all wore their long flowing black gowns. Jo noticed the head scout turning away any student who wasn't wearing the correct formal dress for dinner. The long, oak refectory style tables in hall were lined up in four rows stretching up to the dons' High Table, which ran across the far end on its low dais beneath the portrait of the college founder. There was a huge stone fireplace, in front of which the choristers sang carols after the latin grace, and the meal went ahead more or less according to plan, except for a brief few minutes when the undergraduates picked up on the festive mood and threw bread rolls at each other. The children, on the other hand, were so excited to be waited on and served by the college scouts, that they were quiet and remarkably well-behaved. As a reward for their impeccable behaviour, the scouts said, Father Christmas would soon be paying them a visit.

Back in the common room, the evacuees sat round watching a film projected onto a big paper screen. In the film, Santa was arriving at someone's house and entering the drawing room. There was a hush as the children waited to see what presents he would bring, and the figure of Santa began walking towards the camera. Suddenly, a real man dressed as Father Christmas burst through the paper screen, laden with presents for the children. There were screams of laughter, as fright turned into excitement and the children realised that it was a wonderful practical joke. Jo was delighted to see her new friend happy at last, as Pip smiled and held her hand.

Santa gave each child their own stocking, filled with rag dolls and wooden spoon angels for the girls, and wooden boats or push-along carts or planes for the boys. Every child got a *Pip, Squeak and Wilfred* book, a sugar mouse, an apple and a small, sour orange, into which a hole had been made and sugar poured inside. Jo had never seen children so excited to receive fruit before.

Then, at last, it was time for one final treat before bedtime. Santa promised to take the children to see the deer in Magdalen College Grove, where, he reassured them, some of his own reindeer would be getting their rest, ready for Christmas night. He winked at Jo, and suddenly she realised that the man pretending to be Father Christmas was C.S. Lewis himself.

After searching for their coats, which, of course, Jo didn't have, the children followed 'Santa' out of the college building and into Magdalen Grove. The sky was bright now. The moon was fully up and the clouds had lifted so that the stars shone with diamond brilliance. Jo felt her feet crunching the frost-covered turf.

'Ssssh!' Santa gestured to the children to keep as quiet as they could, as they neared the grove, so as not to startle the deer. Most of the deer had retreated away from them, but in a moment that seemed almost dreamlike, one solitary stag came up quite close to them, as if it were the only animal in the world. It was so magical, that Pip slipped his hand out of Jo's, as if he didn't need her anymore.

Right on cue, Jo felt her phone vibrating: time for her to return to the present.

She moved away from the group. Although aware of the biting cold, she scurried to some bushes and slipped off the shoes, dress and yellow cardigan. Shivering quite violently, she dialled 15800 but just as she pressed the red button, she caught sight of an odd shape glittering on the frosty grass. She bent down to get a closer look. There it was – a brown, knitted toy monkey wearing a sparkly bow-tie. Instinctively, she bent down to pick up the toy. The far-off whine, that she had heard on the journey out, was coming closer and closer. It began to ring in her ears with painful intensity and then…Nothing.

She arrived back in her own bedroom. Everything was exactly the same. Except that Sparkle, the white socks and the blue ribbons had come with her.

CHAPTER 8

The Anderson Shelter
Christmas Cake

In the first few days after Jo had arrived home from her momentous journey back to 1939, home had never felt warmer or cosier, especially since her much loved Grandma Shirley had come to stay for a few days. Everyone noticed how happy Jo was and how much nicer she was being to Oliver.

Jo realised, that although she had met C.S.Lewis, J.R.R.Tolkien and sat in on an Inklings meeting, and even though she had attended the best Christmas party she had ever been to in her life, there was no doubt whatsoever that Dorothy in the *Wizard of Oz* was right: 'there's no place like home'. She remembered, as well, the atmosphere of wartime darkness and the sadness of families being separated, that had been lurking behind all the gaiety. She kept wondering how Pip had coped with the war, without his monkey and away from his parents. She had made a promise to herself to take really good care of Sparkle, as if that in some way made up for having uprooted him from the time period in which he was supposed to exist. Would Pip have found him, she wondered if she hadn't picked him up? So the toy now lived at the bottom of her bed, sat next to her old teddy bear on top of a duvet cover decorated with musical notes and guitars.

'Daydreaming again, Jo?' Grandma Shirley asked. 'This is a new thing, isn't it? I hadn't had you down as a daydreamer before now.'

Jo's parents were out that Saturday afternoon and Grandma was looking after them. 'Sorry Grandma – just a few late nights – no big deal,' Jo fibbed. In fact, she had been feeling the strange-not-quite-there feeling that kept coming over her ever since her return.

Grandma looked at her keenly, in a manner that reminded Jo of Professor Tolkien when he hadn't been completely taken in by her.

'No really, Grandma,' Jo added. 'I'm a bit tired – that's all.'

'Well, I've got a treat in store,' Grandma said, cheerfully. 'Something to perk you up. If we start now, we should just have time to finish before Ollie's four o'-clock rehearsal in College.'

'What is it, Grandma?' asked Oliver, suddenly paying attention now that treats were being mentioned.

'Something that made me laugh when I was a child. Cheered me up during those bleak war years. And Jo's been asking me so many questions lately about World War 2 that I thought we just had to do this. Come with me.' Jo and Oliver exchanged glances each excited to find out what Grandma's special treat could be.

Grandma led them into the kitchen where she had laid out some ingredients on the table.

'We're going to make the Christmas cake this year,' she announced.

'Wow!' said Ollie.

'Brilliant,' said Jo.

They weren't allowed in the kitchen very often, even though they begged Harriet to let them help out more with the cooking. Harriet was far too much of a perfectionist to allow children to mess up her perfectly timed and flavoured menus.

'I don't know why your mother's so possessive of the kitchen,' Grandma said. 'When I was your age...'

'Don't start, Grandma,' Ollie warned.

'Fair enough. Sorry darling,' Grandma laughed. 'I'll try not to be a bore. Now – can either of you guess what's unique about this Christmas cake we are going to make?'

'Hard to say just looking at a load of ingredients,' Ollie said.

'True,' replied Grandma. 'But I have given you a big clue. Think World War 2.'

The children were stumped. Then Jo spotted a sheet of paper that Grandma had obviously printed up. There was a picture of cake baked in a strange shape. It looked like a corrugated hut covered in snow.

'I know!' she exclaimed. 'Are we going to make a cake in the shape of…what were they called? Those shelters that people had at the bottom of their gardens. The old lady who lives next door to Ruby, still has one. Oh what are they called?'

'They were called Anderson shelters and you are right, Jo. Well done! We are going to bake an Anderson Shelter Christmas Cake. I'll never forget the day we baked one with our mother, your great grandma. My sisters and I couldn't stop laughing. And we never felt scared of the shelter again after that. It showed us that even the raids and the misery of nights spent in a damp, dark shelter could have their funny sides. Such a good idea!'

Jo picked up the recipe and studied it, noticing that the picture and instructions had come from a wartime copy of *Good Housekeeping* magazine. She read the sheet aloud to Oliver:

'*The Anderson Shelter is a byword with most of us now and makes an amusing topical subject for a cake, especially if there are children in the family.* That's you and me Ollie. *Bake the cake mixture in an oblong mould or small bread tin and allow to cool, then cover each side with a layer of marzipan, cutting a small 'door' out of the front piece. Next, cut and fix a piece right over the top, marking corrugations with a skewer. Gather the trimmings and knead in enough cocoa to make the colour of earth, and bank them up against the sides of the shelter...* You're right, Grandma, it sounds fun.' Jo put the recipe down.

'Go on reading Jo,' said Grandma. 'Ollie and I will start on the cake mixture.' Grandma weighed out the butter and sugar into a large mixing bowl. Then she handed the bowl to Ollie who began very vigorously mixing the two together with a wooden spoon.

'Steady on Ollie,' said Grandma. 'We want the mixture in the bowl, not all over the table. Carry on Jo.'

'*Finally, cover with a layer of snow made by melting 6 or 8 white marshmallows and pouring over.*' Grandma held up a bag of marshmallows and Ollie put his wooden spoon down to rub his tummy and roll his eyes.

Jo continued: '*Leave a clearing in front of the 'shel-*

ter' for a path and sprinkle with finely chopped, toasted almonds to imitate gravel.'

'Well read, Jo,' said Grandma. 'Now you can start
making the marzipan. Here's my recipe for that. I'm
not going to weigh out the ground almonds and sugar

for you. You're old enough to do it yourself, but I will help you with the egg white.'

The time went by really quickly as the three of them weighed out ingredients, mixed, stirred, tasted and finally put the finished cake in the oven. It would need to cook before they could go on to the most exciting part, adding the decorations.

'What do you think mum and dad will think of it, Grandma?' Jo asked. 'Won't they be wondering why we're making a World War 2 Christmas cake in 2010?'

'Educational, darlings,' Grandma answered. 'And I'll tell them that just for a change, you're sharing a part of *my* life. It's usually the other way round, isn't it?'

Once the cake was baked, Grandma set off with Oliver for Choral Evensong at Magdalen. Jo was expecting Emily and Ruby for a band rehearsal but for a short while there was going to be no one else in the house. She was quite pleased about this as her phone was vibrating in the way she now recognised as SHARP getting in touch. She raced up to her bedroom and shut the door. When she pressed the black button the brilliant blue screen came on and hovered just a few feet away from the phone.

'Good timing, SHARP', she said out loud. 'No one in the house to disturb us.' She felt a surge of excitement as she read Mela's message on the screen – she was about to find out how she had done on her trip:

Hello Jo. This is Mela. I Hope you aren't getting the time slip feeling too badly.
Remember to focus hard on your immediate environment, on what you can see, hear, smell and touch if the symptoms are bad. That should help to stabilise you in the present. If you go to your computer I can send you messages just the same as on your phone and you can type in your messages for me..

Jo went over and switched her computer on. The same message that had been on her phone filled the screen and at the bottom there was a button on which the words: 'post your reply' appeared. She sat down and typed quickly, surprised to find how nervous she was:

'So – how did I do?'

We got some amazing material from you, Jo. There were two problems, though. But don't worry too much about these. Overall, most of the pictures were very good.

'Oh no! What kind of problems?' Jo typed in.

Please don't worry too much, Jo. Our Professor, Aurelia Dobbs has still given me good marks for our work. Just a couple of things you need to be careful about next time.
But as I said, you made the most of the journey. We were delighted with lots of the material.

For a moment, Jo felt like a failure, mortified that she had made some kind of mistake. She had no idea what it might have been.

'Just tell me what I did wrong,' she typed, hesitating before hitting the 'post your reply' button.

Well – there was nothing you could have done about the first thing. It just happened – we're not sure why. Some of your sound and pictures were much clearer than others: usually that depends on how well you fit into the time and place and how the people you meet respond to you. If they don't believe in you, it messes with the transmission.

'Don't tell me – Professor Tolkien?' queried Jo,

her heart sinking as she remembered the feeling she had had that he might in some way have suspected her.

You got it, Jo. Sometimes, when he was in the same room — if he was watching you too closely, the pictures would turn a little hazy. We have no idea why — not even Professor Dobbs. Everything was very clear unless he was focussing on you. She thinks it may have been that he believed in the possibility of time travel — maybe even had experience of it himself. But we've no way of knowing. But it's not a big deal, Jo. That wasn't your fault. And we could still see and hear enough in those pictures to get what we needed. The Arts Department of SHARP is very excited about The Inklings material.

'But I did something wrong too, didn't I?'

Stop beating yourself up, Jo! Most of what you did was excellent — top marks stuff. And this is team work remember? I may not have made things clear enough to you. The thing was, you were a little exposed when you signalled that you were ready to leave. Also, when you press the red return button, you need to have taken off all the clothes from the period in the past. You didn't take the socks off or take the ribbons out of your hair and you were holding something. With those extra things coming back with you, it took more energy to return you safely and it's because of that, that you are feeling time slip quite badly.

Jo felt terrible. Of course, she knew that she had forgotten to take off the socks and the ribbons: she still had them upstairs in her bedroom. She had been so anxious to return, she hadn't hidden herself properly from the others when she had dialled 15800 and pressed the red button to go. And then finding Sparkle had totally thrown her.

'I'm so sorry, Mela. I let you down. I can't believe I forgot to take off the socks and ribbons. And you did tell me to make sure I was hidden from view. I messed up,' she typed.

Luckily we got away with it, Jo. The evacuees were so excited seeing the stag, and their chaperones too, that nobody noticed you go. Everyone was too busy watching the deer. And it was dark, thank goodness, so that helped too. We had a lucky escape. But please, please remember to hide from view next time.

It's essential that no one sees you leave.

'So – there will be a next time? Even though I made such a bad mistake?'

If you could see me now, Jo – I'm laughing! You need to do some work on your self-image, your self-esteem! You are funny, you know. Let me tell you this: we all think you are a natural time traveller. Born to do it. We are hoping you'll agree to another trip.

'Whoopee! You betcha!, typed Jo, so fired up and excited now that she didn't feel like a complete loser.'

Great! I'll take that as a formal 'yes'. You'll be hearing from us again soon.

'That's wonderful, Mela. Thanks so much. Can't wait.'

After that, the screen went blank and Jo switched off her computer.

There was a sudden knock on the door and Jo nearly jumped out of her skin. She was so full of Mela and SHARP and the whole time travel experience that she hadn't even noticed anyone come into the house. Her friends burst into the room.

'What's up Jo?' Ruby exclaimed. 'Band rehearsal, remember? Looks like you forgot!'

'We're playing at the Christmas disco in like, less than two weeks. Hello? Earth calling Jo! Do you even care?' Emily moaned.

Jo took a deep breath. If she didn't bring herself completely back to the present and root herself in her immediate surroundings, she'd get the time slip again. It wasn't a pleasant sensation, so she beamed a radiant smile at her friends.

'Of course I care! How could you even doubt me? And I've got a brilliant idea.'

She had only just noticed that her brother was back from Evensong and that his friends were with him. She could hear them singing in his bedroom, as if they too were still in that ethereal 'chorister space' and like her, hadn't quite come back down to earth yet.

'You know what. I've never asked him this before, but let's go and get some singing tips from Ollie and his mates. Let's go and see the experts! Let's get you some help, Emily!'

CHAPTER 9

On Top Of The World

It was in Blackwell's bookshop the following Monday after school, that SHARP contacted Jo again with instructions for her second trip back in time. She had just had a text from her father saying that he was held up at work and would not be able to meet her as usual. She had decided that she would still have a browse among the books and was sitting in a quiet corner idly leafing through the pages of a supernatural teen thriller, when she felt her phone vibrating with the now familiar quick staccato pulse.

She checked around her – this time she would be *extremely* careful not to let anyone see her – and with no one around, she flicked open the phone and watched the screen turn a vivid blue. She had positioned herself carefully behind a bookshelf with a good view of her bit of the shop, so that if anyone approached her, she would have plenty of time to switch the phone off. Every day, she packed SHARP's small, flat, brown time/space travel bag in her school rucksack just in case she should hear from them while she was out.

She was ready for anything and desperate to get it right – there must be no mistakes from now on!

She steadied her hand, shaking slightly from nerves, keyed in 15800, and pressed the black button. As before, the screen enlarged to around the size of an exercise book. Jo checked again that no one had come towards her quiet corner and then read her message:

Hello Jo. We are all excited about your next trip. Here are your instructions.

‹Details of Current Travel Option›

‹Time Zone›
May 1st, 1945

‹Place›
Magdalen College, Oxford

‹Landing›
The steps leading up to the top of Magdalen Tower

‹Instructions›
Get dressed, then wait to join the appropriate group

‹Destination›

The top of the Tower

‹Identity›

Blend in with your group. Try to stay anonymous

‹Conditions›

With only days to go until Victory in Europe – the end of the war in Europe – the mood is jubilant, upbeat, though many people have lost loved ones in the war. Rationing and poverty are still facts of life.

‹Equipment›

Mobile phone, travel bag. Mobile phone fitted with beam of light activated when t-o-r-c-h is keyed in (only use sparingly)

If you wish to travel, do as follows:
›   wear swimming costume
›   press the time/space travel bag close to your body so that it is attached: key in 15800
›   press the green button to go.
Have a good trip.

Jo wondered if she could go into the Blackwell's loo to change into her swimming costume; she didn't think there would be enough time to get back home – and in any case her mother would be in and it might be difficult to escape to her bedroom. She smiled at the thought of changing, and then time travelling, in such a public place, a bit like being a spy making a contact. Once in the Blackwell's bathroom, she chose a toilet near the wall, it seemed safer somehow, locked the door and started taking off her school uniform. She packed it neatly into her school bag. Then she climbed into her swimming costume and fixed the time/space bag securely to her tummy. She was pleased that she had put Sparkle, the monkey, into her school rucksack. For some reason, she sensed it was important he came with her on the trip.

But why were SHARP sending her back to Magdalen College again? It seemed that whatever she did, in the past or in her present life, she somehow couldn't get away from the place! And interesting that she had been sent first to the beginning of World War 2, and would now experience its end. Why? Well – she would never find out unless she pressed the green button. Here goes, she thought. She confidently hit the green button and then braced herself. Just as before, she heard the strange high-pitched sound coming nearer and nearer, and then...Nothing.

Jo realised she had closed her eyes and when she opened them, she was sitting, just as SHARP had said she would be, at the bottom of the steps of Magdalen College Tower. It was dark, probably just before dawn, she guessed, and chilly, though nothing compared to that biting late afternoon in the wardrobe in December 1939.

Her clothes were in plain view this time. They were in a neat bundle on the step just below the one she was sitting on. As she reached out towards the bundle, her heart gave a leap. *It can't be*! she thought. For the bundle contained some garments that were all too familiar, yet never in a million years had she imagined that *she* would be wearing them.

SHARP *can't* be serious, she thought as she reached out for the chorister's robes that her brother wore almost every day of his life in 2010! No way, Mela! What are you going to make me do? And then it struck her: May 1st, 1945. *May 1st*! This was the day that Magdalen choristers always sang at the top of Magdalen Tower to welcome in the dawn, to celebrate the coming of the light, just as they had for hundreds of years! And what could be more dramatic than a festival of light, just days away from Victory in Europe! Jo was about to take part in an ancient tradition that on this day of this momentous year, would surely banish the darkness of the war forever.

Jo dressed hastily, almost beside herself with excitement. She was going to be a chorister for a day! And what would Emily say? Her friend would be green with envy. And what about Ollie? Would he ever have believed it? The image of Ollie and his friends, who had given Jo and her friends a singing training session only days before, brought Jo down to earth with a bump: they were boys: she was a girl. How on earth was she going to pull this off? Surely they'd rumble her, just as Tolkien had, and then SHARP's pictures would turn out all hazy again. Jo felt the panic rising in her: she didn't want to mess up this time. Surely Mela could have found a better role for her than this?

At that moment, just as Jo was wiping away the tears of frustration, she noticed that there was one last item in a small, velvet bag that had come with the chorister's robes. With trepidation, she opened it and pulled out – scissors!

Oh my god! she thought to herself. They want me to cut my hair! Just like in a Shakespeare play where the female lead has to disguise herself as a boy. Jo perked up instantly: well, SHARP must have a sense of humour, and if they think I can pull this off, then I'll go for it! She reached for the scissors, grabbed the long, fair pony-tail she had worn for as long as she could remember, and cut it off. Then she changed into the chorister's robes, hid Sparkle in the undergarments under the choirboy cassock, and got the thin silver disc out of the travel bag. Just as before, she pressed it to her forehead, put her mobile, her severed ponytail and outer case of the disc back into the bag and hugged the bag to the side of her body. Now all she had to do was wait.

Then, as if from nowhere, there was a flurry and a swish of robes as the choristers arrived, eager to make their way up the steep, circular stone stairs. The Head Chorister looked about her age – twelve and a half she guessed – and to her surprise he looked vaguely familiar. He led the way, not in the least fazed to see her waiting there, and Jo simply fell in with the group as if it were the most natural thing in the world. She realised the boys would be so excited and focused on their big moment – the most important day of the year in any Magdalen chorister's calendar – that they would hardly be wondering if they had a girl in their midst.

'Quick! Get in line!' someone called to her, and

then they were off.

At the top of the stairs was a short ladder and a narrow door leading out onto the roof. She gasped as the sudden breath-taking beauty of the dawn over Oxford struck her senses. The pale first light was making way for the rising sun, its fingers beginning to touch the spires and roofs of the city. If she looked over the parapet she could see the curved High street, as yet undisturbed by traffic, and beneath the tower, a gathered crowd, hushed and waiting. Others, from where Jo stood, appeared like small Lilliputian people as they bobbed about in punts on the Cherwell river. Over towards the east of the city, were trees and meadows – nature in peaceful contrast to the air of expectancy of the human spectators below.

Soon various members of town and gown had assembled on the duckboards – assorted dignitaries who seemed to have special tickets for the occasion. And then the choristers took their places ready to sing.

In the collegiate calendar, winter ended and spring began on the 1st of May. Jo had once been told by her father that, in ancient Rome, the transition had been marked by dances and processions in honour of Flora, goddess of flowers. In Oxford, it was celebrated with hymns and bells. Jo had often been present at her brother's May Day mornings, but always down in the streets with her friends. Never had she felt the atmosphere to be as electrifying as it was today. It was as if the whole city could feel the impending end to the war, and was waiting to burst out into song.

After a final of flutter of noise in the street, a hush fell again as the great college bell struck six, and then Jo opened her mouth, ready to join in with the choir. She was amazed to find that she knew all of the hymns, prayers and madrigals. She had listened to Ollie singing them so often, that she was confident with all of the words and melodies. Surely, she would blend in well enough? Certainly, none of the choirboys had noticed that there was anything different about her. I must be a convincing boy, she smiled to herself as she heard herself trilling *Te Deum Patrem Colimus* (Thee God the Father We Worship), a hymn derived from the Latin graces of the college. Next up was a Vaughan Williams setting of an old English folk tune, and so it went on, with Jo's confidence as a treble growing with every hymn, prayer and madrigal that they performed. And then at last, as the glorious harmonies ended, the great ten bells of Magdalen tower began to ring, making Jo's ears pound and the ground tremble beneath her.

She felt as if she was standing on top of the world, with a sea of sky above and an ocean of sound below, and the city stretched out at her feet. It was over all too soon. The sun had risen, the traffic and bicycles started to move again on the streets and the punts on the river, and the groups of pedestrians far below began to break up and move away.

Jo took one last look down and around before she followed the other choirboys down the dark spiral stairs, past the resounding clamour of the bell-chamber, which seemed to shake the whole tower, and then out into the college once more.

Her feet on solid ground at last, Jo realised she now felt slightly faint and dizzy. The noise of the bells had been almost deafening. She was relieved when someone pulled her sleeve and the physical sensation seemed to snap her out of a trance.

'Hey,' said a voice at her side. 'Fancy skipping breakfast in college and taking a punt on the river with me?'

Jo turned to see the boy of her age waiting eagerly for her response. It was the chorister who had looked vaguely familiar.

'They won't notice we've gone, you know', he added. 'Any other May Day morning they would, but

this war's only going to end once, you know. Let's celebrate!'

CHAPTER 10

Sparkle Finds His Way Home

Jo breathed in the heady scent of the May morning. She turned to her new companion:

'I'd love to.' she answered him. 'But don't you think they'll spot us leaving?'

'Hang back with me for a moment,' the boy advised. 'They won't wait for anyone.'

He was right: the other choristers hurried towards the dining hall, keen to get their hands on their hard-earned breakfasts, while Jo and her friend tucked themselves out of sight to let the college dignitaries file past them.

'We've got to get to the buttery now. Carrie, the scout's put aside a picnic hamper for me, and a portable wind-up gramophone, so we can listen to some music on the river,' he confessed. 'You see, we had it all planned, my friend Tom was going to come, but he's down with laryngitis, so that's why I asked you. I'm Carrie's favourite, you know. She'd do anything for me.'

'Won't she get into trouble if they find out?' asked

Jo, concerned for the servant's job.

'Not today! Half the university's joining in the celebrations. Everyone knows there'll be victory in Europe any day now.'

Just in time, Jo stopped herself from saying: 'eight days away to be exact.' She remembered her promise, she must blend in; not reveal that she had foreknowledge of events.

Carrie the scout, who Jo recognised as the servant who had collected her from Staircase 3, Room 3 that momentous day in 1939, had kept her promise and was waiting to one side of the buttery door for her secret rendezvous with the chorister.

'Here, Master Philip,' she whispered. The woman handed over a basket covered with a white linen cloth to her young friend and then the portable gramophone with a few 78 records to Jo. Underneath her servant's cap, her face looked much the same as it had five and a half years ago – a little older, perhaps, but otherwise unchanged. Jo smiled to herself as she realised that she would be the only person here who hadn't aged at all. But how funny that she was now disguised as a boy and had chopped off her hair!

'Thanks Carrie,' Philip said, warmly. 'You're a gem.'

Jo knew they would hardly be inconspicuous leaving Magdalen College carrying a gramophone and a picnic hamper and still dressed in their chorister robes, but she realised Philip was right: the mood she could sense out in the city was so ebullient that, for once, no one was going to mind what anybody else was doing. She remembered Grandma talking about VE day itself: the parties in the streets, the crowds flooding into the town squares, waving flags and banners. Now she too was a part of this joyful month in 1945.

They hurried over the grass of the quad, gleaming like a green jewel in the morning sunlight, and then out of the college and onto the streets of Oxford. It seemed to Jo as if they were suddenly hit by an explosion of sound and colour. They almost got tangled up in a troupe of Morris dancers prancing about in white shirts and trousers, green cross belts and rosettes, and bells at their knees. One man played a concertina as the men whirled around, waving a white handkerchief in each hand, and then swapping them for long sticks for the more vigorous dances. Jo and Philip stayed to watch an old man's solo dance. He was dressed in white like the others, but with red cross belts.

As well as the bright pageantry and medieval confusion that was a traditional part of the May morning celebrations in Oxford, Jo breathed in the delights of the Oxford summer – Trinity term, as it was still known in 2010. Summer frocks and black gowns darted about like butterflies and moths through the city streets, flowers danced in the college gardens and Oxford's trees almost seemed to burst with new buds before her eyes. Bicycles rang their bells as they raced over ancient stone and gramophones joined in the cacophony from the water-ways at Magdalen Bridge.

Jo and Philip fought their way through the crowds who had come out, all eager to be part of the May morning festivities, and at last won their fight to hire a punt, as they jostled for position in the queue.

Companionably, they took it in turns to punt, using the huge pole to stop themselves going round in circles.

'Who taught you to punt so well?' Jo asked her new friend.

'Just practise, I've plenty of time for it in the holidays,' Philip replied modestly. 'You're not bad yourself, you know. It's the strangest thing, but we've been singing together all this time and I don't even know your name. And I'm sure I know all the other boys' names!'

'It's Jo, silly,' Jo laughed. 'Remember?'

At that moment, they were interrupted by a cry of: 'Look ahead!' as another punt, carrying a party that looked very Edwardian to Jo, almost bumped into them. Jo noticed how the grey flannels and tweed jackets of the winter war months had been replaced with the summer wear - grey flannels but with cricket shirts and college blazers for the men and bright, thin cotton frocks for the women.

Somehow, Jo and Philip managed not to get their punt pole stuck in the mud. Jo had often been on the river in her own time and watched helpless punters left hanging onto their poles while the punts went gliding on without them and other passengers frantically tried to paddle back to rescue them. But their morning on the river went without a hitch. Other boats passed them, often shouting out to them, amused to see two choristers on the river in full regalia. But Jo and Philip held their own, ate their picnic and listened to the swing records that Carrie had packed for them on their wind-up gramophone, which every boat seemed to have as an essential. The strains of 'Love in Bloom' mixed with the likes of Benny Goodman, Artie Shaw and Bob Crosby, while an endless procession of boats passed by: outriggers, canoes, two-pair tubs, pair-oar skiffs and punts – punts, punts and still more punts.

Jo and Philip didn't talk much, preferring instead to play their ten inch 78 records in their paper covers, stamped with the name of the shop from which they were bought. But finally Jo thought she ought to ask him: 'where are your parents, Philip? Won't they be wondering where you are?'

Philip's expression suddenly clouded over. 'Lost them in a bombing raid,' he answered, tersely.

Jo felt bad that she had put her foot in it, but how could she have known? As if he could read her thoughts, Philip tried to reassure her. 'Don't worry – you didn't mean anything.'

Jo blushed. 'Well – what about the people who look after you now? Do you need to get home to them?'

'Been with the same family since I came here as an evacuee. Never thought it would be forever.'

'I'm so sorry, Philip. I shouldn't have said anything,' Jo replied, struggling to find the right words, but she needn't have worried. Philip suddenly wanted to talk.

'One night, we were allowed to go up onto the

college roof with the firewatchers. It was a beautiful night. 1940. Clear skies and plenty of stars. Then we saw this incredible, strong glow of orange, growing and spreading over the horizon. This was different: it wasn't like the nights when the raids on London reflected on the clouds forty miles away. I sort of knew. I had this terrible feeling in my tummy. Next morning, we found out it was the burning of Coventry. Both my parents died.'

'Oh no!' was all Jo could bring herself to reply. Some understanding of the endless darkness of the war came back to haunt her, as if the shadow of it had never really gone away, had been lurking behind the brightness of this May morning all along. This must be how her Grandma felt, even now. It was true when people said that there are some things that can never be forgotten.

'What did you do then, Philip?

'Stayed here in Oxford - became a chorister.'

With a shock, Jo realised that her new twelve-year-old friend, Philip, was also her seven-year-old evacuee friend, Pip: the same person, just five years older and now the same age as her. How blind she had been! She couldn't believe she hadn't noticed before. The toy monkey she still had hidden under her robes might be the only memento he would have of his parents, especially if their home and everything in it had been destroyed in the raid. Would he even remember the toy though, and how could she return it without blowing her cover?

And then – trust SHARP to pick this moment to signal that it was time for her to return! She felt her phone vibrating with its familiar pulse, and an idea struck her as she spotted a barge moored by the riverbank – a houseboat that had empty rooms she had noticed people using to get changed into their bathing costumes. Perfect. She asked Philip to punt towards it, complaining of feeling too hot in her chorister's robes now the sun was high up in the sky. As he focussed all his attention on getting them towards the bank, she chose a moment when he looked away from her, and carefully pulled out Sparkle from under her robes. She placed the monkey gently in the hamper and then spread the cotton cloth over it to hide the toy. Philip was certain to find him later.

Then with a powerful emotion she couldn't even begin to describe, she said a quick 'good bye' to Philip and told him to take the punt back and that she'd find him later. She desperately wanted to give him a hug, but knew that he, like Ollie if one of his friend's did that, would think it really strange. She jumped on to the bank as soon as the punt came alongside, gave a quick wave and disappeared into the barge. Once inside, she quickly shed her choristers' robes and left them folded neatly in a pile on the floor. Goodbye 1945, goodbye summer, goodbye Sparkle and goodbye my wonderful new friend, Philip, she thought. Then she took a deep breath, dialled 15800 and pressed the red button. A faint high-pitched whine shrilled in her ears and then…Nothing.

The Coda

Jo stepped out of the Blackwell's loo in 2010 and bumped straight into Stuart – the boy from the covered market.

'Hey!' he exclaimed, genuinely delighted to see her. 'Fab hair, by the way. I was going to call you. I want to coach your band. No charge of course. And I've had a brilliant idea: I think I know how you can turn it into something really different...'

Ten days later at the Christmas Sparkle disco, Harriet and Matthew watched as Stuart led Jo's band out onto the stage. He introduced them under their new name – The Tune Army – consisting of Jo on drums and backing vocals, himself on lead guitar, Ruby on keyboards and Emily on bass guitar and vocals. But there was a twist. To everyone's complete surprise, Ollie and a group of choristers filed onto the stage with them too, though dressed in jeans and T-shirts instead of their usual robes, and lined up in front of some microphones of their own.

'Ladies; gentlemen; rock n' rollers!', Stuart shouted to the curious crowd. 'Welcome to the new choral-rock fusion sound. You heard it here first!' And with that, the band, backed by Ollie's choral singers, burst into life.

Back home later that same night, and still flushed with success, Jo also received her much-anticipated message from Mela:

Thank you Jo for your amazing sound and pictures from 1945.

All perfect this time and no slip-ups! Congrats! No Professor Tolkien to mess with the transmission. I'll be in touch soon.

Take care, Jo, and thanks again.

Yipee!, Jo thought. This has been the best night ever.

And who knows what our Tune Army under Stuart's tuition might go on to do? What a great idea of his to get Ollie and his mates involved. The group really works at last with their involvement.

Jo went and knocked on her brother's bedroom door. She gave him a big hug.

'Thanks, Ollie. You were amazing tonight. I'm sorry I've been such a grumpy sister', she added. 'I think I was just so jealous of you.'

'I know', replied Ollie, a little bit smug but nevertheless glad of Jo's apology. 'But I've always been jealous of your freedom: no rehearsals and performances, and having to carry the reputation of Magdalen College choir on your shoulders. And never having to worry if you catch a cold, or eat chocolate, or have a late-night sometimes. It isn't always fun, you know.

But of course it's all worth it in the end.'

'And I know now how hard you work on the singing too, Ollie', Jo continued. 'It's a lot of pressure for a ten year old. You really are a star, you know. And thanks for singing with my band. Weren't we brilliant?'

At that moment, Jo heard Harriet calling her name from downstairs.

'Better go,' she said. 'Mum doesn't like to be kept waiting!'

As Jo walked into her mother's study, Harriet threw her arms around her. 'I was so proud of you tonight', she said. 'Not so sure about the hair cut, but I'll let that go...But I'm so proud!'

Jo tried not to look amazed. As she beamed a big smile back at Harriet, she caught sight of a book on her mother's shelf that she hadn't ever noticed before: *The Lost Road* by J.R.R.Tolkien.

'What's that book about?' she asked.

'Well – it's Tolkien's time travel story,' her mother replied. 'A less well known work than his *Lord of the Rings* trilogy, or *The Hobbit*. But it's one of my favourites. And Tolkien was a member of a famous literary group called The Inklings, who met in C.S.Lewis's rooms in Magdalen in the 1930's and 40's...'

Jo interrupted her: 'Yes – I know all that, mum.'

'Do you?!' exclaimed Harriet, surprised.

'Can I borrow that book?' Jo asked. 'I'd like to read it.' Harriet looked at her daughter as if she was seeing her for the first time.

Thanks and Acknowledgements

With thanks to my family - Andy, Rachel and Ethan, and my mother, Patricia Horne - for all their encouragement, and also to Oxford archivist Robin Darwall-Smith and Clare Ferguson of Magdalen College School for their help, advice and support.

The following publications were also valuable for research purposes:

Oxford Today - The University Magazine
Good Housekeeping Magazine
J.R.R. Tolkien and C.S.Lewis - The Story of Their Friendship by Colin Duriez
C.S.Lewis - The Authentic Voice by William Griffin
Oxford At War by John Harper-Nelson

And finally:

Dorothy L.Sayers novel, Gaudy Night, provided inspiration as did Archie Young's Observer magazine article about his time as a chorister at Westminster Abbey.

Competitions And Activities

Seven Arches Publishing often runs competitions for you to enter with prizes of book tokens, that can be spent in any bookshop, for solving puzzles or for a good illustration. Why not go to www.sevenarches-publishing.co.uk and check out whether there is competition or activity on its way based on one or other of our books. We often include the winning entries of our competitions, or the writing, poems or pictures that you send us in the next print run of the title.

Contact Us

You are welcome to contact Seven Arches Publishing by:

Phone: 0161 4257642

Or

Email: admin@sevenarchespublishing.co.uk

Collect other books in the Time Traveller Kids series

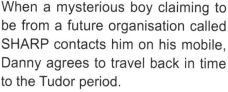

When a mysterious boy claiming to be from a future organisation called SHARP contacts him on his mobile, Danny agrees to travel back in time to the Tudor period.

Danny's interest in history is zero, but somehow making friends in the long forgotten past gets him seriously hooked on time travel.

Incredibly musically gifted, Atlanta is entranced by the music of the far-into-the- future humankind. Is this what makes her agree to join the growing band of twenty first century kids who go back in time to gather information, for the organisation called SHARP?

When Alex McLean is catapulted back to 1314 by a rival outfit to SHARP, his life is in serious danger. They do not care if he falls to his death with the desperate band of Scots fighters who did the impossible and scaled the terrifying Rock on which Edinburgh Castle stands to this day.